JAMES

Gates of Heaven – Book 3

M. Tasia

ALSO BY M. TASIA

The Boys of Brighton series

Gabe

Sam's Soldiers

Rick's Bear

Jesse

Coop

Travis

Grady

Vincent

Shadow

The Holidays

The Gates of Heaven series

Saint

Finn

EVERYONE LOVES THE BOYS OF BRIGHTON

"I loved this book and I love this town. I hope there's going to be more."
—Melissa Lemons on *Gabe*

"An amazing read that was filled with lust, love, crazy hot sex, danger, action and so much more This is the first book I have read in this series but I will definitely be reading more in the future."
—Gay Book Reviews on *Sam's Soldiers*

"I was crazy impressed that the author made me teary over the ending of a relationship that I shouldn't have even been invested in.

I didn't yet know these characters yet the author made me hurt for them. That takes some mad writing skills!"
—Love Bytes Reviews

"Jesse and Royce together have my heart. Jesse has it all by himself."
—The Book Junkie Reads on *Jesse*

"So much action, intrigue, drama and angst for the long awaited story of Grady and Ben. This was worth the wait. Sexy and sweet. I can't wait for the next."
—SamD on *Grady*

"I knew this one would be my favorite to date! There was something about Vincent that said awesome then came Tristan."
—Booky on *Vincent*

"This installment of the Boys of Brighton was so good! I loved Shadow and Randy 's story I was hooked from the first page to the last. This book was definitely worth the wait!"
—AG on *Shadow*

"I have loved this series from the very first story and this holiday novella is simply perfect. We get a glimpse of all our couples and what is happening in their lives while the holidays explode around them. I cannot wait for more!"
—bookobsessed on *The Holidays*

EVERYONE'S NEWEST LOVE – THE GATES OF HEAVEN

"Having read the entire Boys of Brighton series, I was eagerly awaiting Saint's story and it was so worth the wait. I enjoyed every word. I am always amazed by authors that bring characters to life so much that you can hardly wait for the next story. Cannot wait for Finn and Miguel to have their turn. While I'm waiting I'll reread the Boys of Brighton series!" —Debbie Kay on *Saint*

"Ms. Tasia has done it again! This is Saint's story, for readers of the Brighton Boys, you'll know he needs a break! After being forced to become a plastic surgeon by his father, he rebels by assisting people in 3rd world countries, which puts him in the position to be kidnapped and tortured. You really feel for him, that's for sure! Max is the perfect man for poor Saint's battered soul, not that he doesn't have his own issues! Overall, this was engaging, steady paced and chock full of all the feels!" —Avid Reader on *Saint*

"Finn and Miguel stole my heart. This is a great Sunday afternoon read. Finn's character jumped off the page as his story developed through each chapter. I loved reading his truth and watching him and Miguel find their home in each other." —K.A. Brown on *Finn*

"Another tale from the Gates of Heaven, another two brilliant MCs we get to know very well. I loved both the plot and the characters, all their emotions and insecurities on full display. All the descriptions and world building were very vivid, providing a great background for an emotional story of self discovery and developing attraction." —AL on *Finn*

www.BOROUGHSPUBLISHINGGROUP.com

JAMES
Copyright © 2019 M. Tasia

ISBN 978-1-951055-28-8

This has been possible because of the love and support of my family. Love you Craig, Samantha, Katie, and Jason.

ACKNOWLEDGMENTS

Thank you to my amazing publisher for taking the time to play tour guide in her diverse and stunning area of Southern California. Your indomitable spirit and strength inspires me to continue to grow as an author. Also, to my sisters-in-law, thank you for coming along and supporting my dream. The love and strength of family is the cornerstone of my career.

JAMES

PROLOGUE

The amber liquid burned his throat as he swallowed, exactly the way he liked it. James scanned the crowd, as he'd done dozens of times since he'd arrived. The bar was busy with groups celebrating whatever the latest occasion was, or singles looking to hook up, trolling the crowds hoping to find a happy diversion.

James didn't fit into either category. He wanted to be left alone to drink in peace and watch storylines play out in front of him from his corner booth. The intentional deep-set scowl should've been enough to keep people away, but there were those men and women who took it as a challenge. Get the big grumpy guy to smile, one point. Laugh, two points. And so on.

James sat in his booth, ignoring the latest make-him-happy applicant until they finally gave up and left. Why was it so hard for people to understand he didn't want to be social, didn't want sex, and he sure the hell wasn't looking for a boyfriend.

Peace. That was what he wanted most of all. Which sort of begged the question, what the hell was he doing in the middle of a noisy bar?

He picked up his glass, drained the remainder of his whiskey, and motioned at the server for another. It had been a month since he'd found his brother, Finn, at the receiving end of a gun their papa was pointing at him and his lover. James had given their crazy bastard father a chance to stand down, but the asshole was beyond reasoning. He was forced to kill his father in the middle of the woods, on a dark and moonless night.

As if that wasn't enough to get him into the Guilt Olympics, his continued nightmares of what he'd seen through four tours of deployment played like a movie through his mind the moment his lids dropped. It wasn't enough that he'd been left with a few bullet holes for his service, but now it appeared that PTSD had moved in. James wasn't a roommate kind of guy.

"Here you go." Peggy dropped off his double shot of whiskey. "How you feeling tonight?"

Peggy, one of the owners of Crandall's Pub, had taken one look at James and decided he was her latest project. The only reason he hadn't left and found a new watering hole was that the older woman had a huge heart, and she got that twinkle in her eye every time she was cooking something up that had nothing to do with a kitchen. Tonight was no different. She patiently waited for him to reply.

"I'm okay."

"Have you been getting enough sleep?"

"Not in years. The enemy always waits for a moment of weakness."

"But you're not in the Army anymore. You need to find a way to deal with it and move on. Have you thought about seeing a therapist?"

Of course it had crossed his mind, but something was holding him back. "I have, and I'm still thinking on it."

Peggy reached out to cover James's much larger hand. "Okay, honey. But if you need anything, me and Henry are always here to help."

"Thank you." He hoped that'd end the conversation.

He didn't need to bring any more innocent people into his messed-up world.

She sighed as if she could tell what he was thinking, but accepted his reply with a nod before turning away to take someone else's order.

James wrapped his hand around the glass to steady himself. He was already on his fourth drink and had no plans on stopping anytime soon. The building where he was staying was only three blocks away. He could stumble that far.

The bell over the front door of the pub rang, causing James to look up. He groaned loud and long, not caring if the new arrival heard him or not. Once that crystal blue gaze landed on him, James knew he was screwed.

Why wouldn't this guy take the hint and leave him alone? Was he a glutton for punishment or plain stupid-stubborn? James didn't know, but the bastard was headed in this direction with the same damn smile plastered on his puss he always wore. Shit.

His long legs ate up the distance, and without so much as a *May I?,* he slid into the booth beside James.

"Hey, good looking, you come here often?"

James almost smiled. Almost. Peggy dropped off a black coffee and continued on her way with a knowing look.

"You can stuff that line up your ass, Ross. I'm not in the mood for your shit."

"Is that any way to talk to your ride home?"

"I'll walk the three damn blocks, if you don't mind."

"I do mind. It's close to two in the morning and Finn has been trying to reach you for hours. Any particular reason you're not answering your phone?"

"Ah, yeah. I want to be left alone."

"Keep this up and you're going to get your wish."

"Go to hell, Ross."

"Already have an express pass. Now finish up your drink so I can get your drunk ass home before your brother calls in the National Guard."

"How does he even know I'm not at the building? It's not like he lives there anymore."

"He and Miguel came over to watch the game with Saint, Max, and you, if your ass had been at home."

"That's not my home."

"Touchy, and don't care. Let's go." Ross swallowed the last of his coffee and stood, waiting for James to join him.

"Whatcha gonna do, arrest me?" James laughed without humor.

Ross reached behind his back and pulled out his handcuffs. "If I have to."

Shit.

James didn't know if he was pissed off or turned on.

CHAPTER 1

"Seriously?" the deep voice snapped at him.

James didn't bother looking out the open window of the squad car. At least he wasn't in the back of it, a fact that the angry detective didn't seem to appreciate.

"You can't be left on your own," Detective Richard Ross, James's self-appointed guardian, groaned. "You're a damn two-hundred-sixty-pound child."

"Two-fifty."

Hell, he wasn't that heavy.

Ross's responding growl made the hairs on the back of James's neck stand at attention. He was quick to run his hand beneath his hairline to quell his overactive libido's rebellion. He needed to get laid soon, because that shit had to stop. He clenched his hands in frustration, sending a shard of pain up his left forearm, not only making him hiss, but also drawing Ross's attention. James knew there was no way to hide the bloody bandages wrapped around his left hand.

"What the hell did you do now?" Ross accused.

Well, shit, he'd called the detective for help, so what the fuck? Had Ross gotten his ass there sooner, the patrol car wouldn't have arrived and made a scene out of an easy cleanup.

Before James had a chance to respond, the responding officer spoke up.

"He didn't like the way a pimp was talking to one of his girls."

"Asshole had it coming. I warned him. Did he listen? No. Not my fault." Plain and simple.

Ross huffed out a deep breath before asking, "Where's the pimp, Officer Webb?"

"Over at Good Samaritan," the cop answered while trying to keep the smirk off his face.

James liked the guy.

"You put him in the hospital?" Ross glared at James in disbelief.

"He hit her, I hit him… yadda, yadda, yadda." Again, plain and simple.

Ross shook his head and turned his attention back to the cop, who was still fighting the lip twitch. That guy understood. Ross, not so much.

"What is he charged with?"

"Nothing," the cop answered. "The pimp wasn't looking to press charges."

"Nothing?" Ross waved his hand toward the police cruiser.

"See, that's what I said," James grumbled as he reached for the door handle. "But my ass is still sitting in this car."

"Sit that ass back down," Ross growled again.

Come to think of it, Ross growled a lot whenever he was around James. Coincidence? Doubtful.

"Bossy."

"Word is," Officer Webb said, "if any of us come across a James Masterson to get a hold of you, Detective." He adjusted his bulletproof vest.

James knew how uncomfortable those things could be when the sun beat down on you.

"What the fuck? You're having me watched?" This time, James did open the door and step out. "What? Am I some kind of pet project of yours?"

"More like penance for something heinous I must've done in a former life," Ross ground out.

This time Officer Webb couldn't hold back. Laughing he said, "Okay, I can see you have this under control. Maybe you can get him to go in for stitches."

Shaking his head, the cop rounded his patrol car, got in, and drove away, his smile still in place.

"Let's go." Ross ordered, making James bristle.

"Yeah, I don't think so."

James wasn't in the mood for Ross's shit today. He had already dealt with one bossy asshole and look where that got him. With a fight-bite gash from the knuckle of James's index finger to the middle of the back of his hand, and a round of antibiotics in his future. He'd had enough for one day. Hell, the girl had even attacked him after her pimp hit the ground. What the fuck was wrong with people?

Was his tetanus shot up to date? Christ knew what germs and diseases were floating around in that mouth filled with gold-capped teeth. James couldn't help but wonder if the guy could get a refund from his dentist since most of his teeth were lying on the sidewalk. He doubted the teeth would remain on the sidewalk for long, even if the scavengers had to melt the teeth down for the gold.

"What are you smiling about?" Ross asked.

"Nothing. Thinking," James answered. "See you around, Ross."

He made it two damn steps before Ross yelled, "Get your ass in my car before I turn you over my knee."

That stopped him in his tracks at the same time a thrill skated down his spine.

"If you're going to act like a child, then I'll treat you like one," Ross bit out. "Now get in the police car like a good little boy and let the nice police officer take you to the ER, where you might get a lollypop if you behave."

James was gob-smacked, and that didn't happen often. He fought the smile, but for some reason—he knew why, but denial was working overtime—he walked up to the faded standard-issued Crown Vic, reached for the passenger door handle and pulled it open. Wedged between the door and seat—it must've slid in there the first time he got in and out of the car—was the polka-dotted canvas lunch bag, and it fell onto the sidewalk in front of him.

James picked it up between his thumb and forefinger as if it might explode.

"Getting in touch with your feminine side? Don't get me wrong, you do you, but I never pictured you as a polka-dot kinda guy."

Damn, James was about to laugh. A smile and a laugh not only in one day, but minutes apart. The apocalypse was coming.

"Toss it into the backseat," Ross told him, without so much as a smirk.

James did as he was told before getting into the passenger seat, but he was far from done. Curiosity had always been one of his many fatal flaws. As a kid, his father had whipped his back so many times, by the time James was ten, he'd hardly noticed the pain.

He continued to stare at the detective's profile, noticing the grey threading through Ross's dark hair.

Ross turned to look at him. "My niece made lunch for me. She's five."

James backed off, holding in his grin, then turned his attention out the window to the delivery truck backing into an alley a block up the crowded street. The incessant beeping was wearing thin. With a loud huff, Ross pulled away from the curb and James counted down the seconds before the interrogation began.

"What the hell were you thinking starting a fight in the middle of the sidewalk, in broad daylight?"

"I didn't start the fight. I responded to what was put in front of me."

It didn't matter that James had had to cross the street to put the pimp in his path. A little fact he would keep to himself.

"You're telling me you weren't jonesing to knock that pimp into next week?"

"Well, someone had to do something." And he happened to be up for the job.

"You're not some kinda superhero roaming the streets and protecting the public. You can't save everyone."

"Why not. It could be my new shtick."

James grumbled. It was not his intention to become anything approaching a hero. He knew the cost, which was one of the reasons he was way too screwed up to even try.

"No one is capable of protecting everyone one hundred percent of the time. No matter how hard he tries," Ross continued with his admonishing.

James had been treated to a lot of that shit over the last few months.

It bothered him to hear the defeat in Ross's voice, and it sounded as if Ross spoke from experience. But who was he to judge. James had his own truckload of fucked-up to deal with, he had no business questioning someone else's.

"Duly noted, Detective."

The remainder of the drive to the hospital was silent, which James appreciated. He had been fighting back one of his blinding headaches since he'd woken up, and this situation wasn't helping the marching band doing laps in his skull.

Building after building flew by and they became a blur. If he closed his eyes, he was sure he could hear the hum of the Stryker armored vehicle that had become his home for far too many days and nights. The hum from the powerful three-hundred-fifty-horse-powered engine had often been the last sound he heard when falling asleep and first when he woke. Sometimes it was hard to pull away from the memories, no matter how hard he tried.

"James. Hey, man, we're here." Ross shook James by his shoulder.

He looked around as the sea of sand slowly solidified into a building. How long had they been sitting in the reserved police parking spot outside the ER doors? He stared at Ross's crystal blue eyes and was surprised to see concern. That sobered him up faster than the sound of gunfire.

He shrugged off Ross's hand and straightened. "I'm good."

James opened his door and got out before anything else could be said. He moved quickly and didn't stop until he was standing in front of the check-in desk.

James could feel Ross sidle up beside him but refused to look over at the detective. He hadn't lost himself to his memories in someone's presence before. He had worked hard to avoid that from happening. He didn't need anyone to see his crazy.

"How can I help you, Detective Ross?" a freckled-faced young man asked, from the other side of the glass partition.

The guy had to be fresh out of nursing school, because no one who worked in an ER looked that happy after they'd clocked in a few years. James could relate. The sight of trauma day after day dragged the happy out of people.

"My friend needs stitches. He's a grumpy-ass, so you might want to make it fast, Harry." Ross told the kid.

"Hey, I'm right here," James blustered, knowing it made no difference to the annoying detective.

"Yes, you are," Ross shot back.

"This way, gentlemen." Harry instructed and led them to a standard curtained walled room with a triage gurney.

If James wasn't mistaken, the smaller man was adding a little extra shake to those hips with every step.

"The doctor should be in to see you shortly."

James knew that was code for sit and wait, so he did, but not on the gurney. He would never willingly do that again, so he took one of the two chairs.

Harry took the clipboard and placed it on a metal hanger before giving Ross a serious once-over without even trying to hide his desire. James had no idea why that bothered him, and he snapped his brows together. The newbie took one look at James and hightailed it out of the room.

Ross was about to sit when his phone rang, and after he glanced at the screen he moved into the hallway. The concern on his face made James antsy, but the man was a detective. Most of his calls weren't happy, happy. That James even cared to notice was disturbing. He had to get a handle on this.

Since being forced to shoot his father to save his brother's life, the good detective had been James's constant shadow. Or at least, it felt that way. James had asked Finn straight out if he was having the detective watch him, and his brother denied it. James believed him. Over the past three months, he had seen more of the man than his own reflection. James avoided mirrors whenever possible. He didn't need to see the scars to know they were there. It wasn't so much his ego that refused to accept the deep line that ran from his temple to his jaw, it was the memories it evoked.

The curtain pulled back to reveal a sheepish Harry and a taller man in scrubs, who James presumed was the ER doc.

"Hello, Mr. Masterson. I'm Doctor Glazier. Seems you might require stitches. May I see your hand?"

James lifted his arm and held out his hand so the doc could undo the bandage over his wound. He inspected the three-inch gash that ran from the knuckle of James's index finger to the middle of the back of his hand. James was sure the gold crowns had something to do with the extent of the damage. Ross came back in as the doc was finishing his assessment.

"Well, we'll need to take X-rays to make sure there isn't anything broken or fractured. Harry can clean out the wound while we wait on the imaging department. After that, we'll reassess and get you stitched up."

"Thanks, Doc," James replied.

Harry and the doc turned and left him alone with Ross. The man looked pensive.

"What's wrong?" James asked.

Ross clipped his phone onto his belt before answering him. "A guy got out on bail about an hour ago. I'm being kept in the loop."

James was not buying it, but before he had the chance to ask more, Harry came back in with a tray full of supplies. Now, the real fun would begin. The adrenaline had worn off long ago, and James's hand was throbbing something fierce before the nurse dug in.

Over the next two hours, James was poked, prodded, X-rayed, sterilized, and stitched, until he finally found himself back in Ross's car. They headed to The Gates, where he was crashing. Ross had been quiet, and it was unnerving not to hear a lecture, a slew of admonishments, or to be yelled at.

When they pulled into the parking lot behind the building, Ross parked between two of Max's trucks. The construction crews were busy working on the upper floors of the building, where they were converting derelict spaces into condominiums, even as the restaurant, bar, and lounge were preparing to open to the public. Saint'd had a couple soft openings to work out the bugs, but as far as James knew, everything was ready to go.

He walked up the metal back steps and pressed his code into the security panel, unlocking the steel door. He walked through a maze of new shelving loaded down by box after box of supplies. The hub, where they lived temporarily, had been walled-off from the remainder of the first floor, giving the occupants privacy. His space wasn't anything special, a room with bath attached, but it suit him for now.

The moment he stepped into the living room, he knew he was screwed. James glared at Ross as his brother hugged him.

"Rat," James growled at the infuriating man.

"Trouble," Ross replied with a smirk.

Bastard.

Then he had the nerve to whip out a red lollypop. "As promised."

CHAPTER 2

Ross watched as Finn hugged James, while the rest of the crew hung back. Saint, Max, Marian, and Miguel kept their distance, allowing Finn his time with his brother.

Ross didn't care if the colossal pain-in-the-ass thought he was a rat for giving Finn the heads-up about his brother's whereabouts. Hell, James was lucky to have people that cared for him. Unfortunately, he didn't realize it, and if he did, he shunned the care and attention.

Watching the brothers, it seemed there'd be a lengthy discussion in James's future, and Ross had no time to watch the well-deserved tongue-lashing.

"I'm out." Ross turned to James. "Try to stay out of trouble."

If looks could kill, Ross would've been eviscerated. Knowing it would piss-off James, Ross smiled wider.

Finn let James go and came over to hug Ross. "Thank you for taking care of him."

"I'm a damn adult." James ripped the sucker out of Ross's hand, then made fast work of removing the wrapper before shoving it in his mouth.

"Then act like one," Ross demanded. "You take off for days without a word and turn up with bruises and stitches, scaring your brother half to death. I know you've been through hell fighting for our country, and I deeply respect that, but if you're aiming to get yourself killed here at home, don't do it on my patch, asshole."

James had the decency to lose some of his indignation before looking away.

"Later." Ross made tracks to the backdoor and then his car.

He had to get back to the station and find out what the hell went wrong. The cosmos was working against him. Every stoplight felt like an eternity as crowds mingled in the crosswalks. People laughed and talked as if they had all the time in the world. It felt like everyone was shuffling their feet.

A bead of sweat slid down his neck, into the back of his shirt. He was tempted to turn on his interior light bar, but that would be wrong. This might be an emergency to him, but it wasn't an official police emergency.

When Ross finally pulled into the station's garage, he was ready to blow. How could Avante have gotten bail after all the evidence against him? Ross had worked the case for over two years, the "T's" were crossed and every last "I" had a damn dot. The bastard should be rotting in jail while waiting for his trial. He was a proven flight risk and had been implicated in several high-profile murders.

Ross stepped into the elevator, repeatedly pressing the button for his floor, as if that would magically get him to the third floor faster. He didn't wait until the doors opened fully, but sidestepped out and strode right into chaos.

Phones were ringing, and his colleagues seemed to be working feverishly on what he guessed was a new case. There were only six detectives at this stationhouse, so they were a close unit.

"What's going on?" he boomed, to be heard over the din of phones ringing.

The other five turned to him and fell silent. They hung up their phones and ignored the ringing.

Shit.

"Ross... um."

The elevator dinged behind them, stopping Bev, his friend, and sometime-partner, from saying any more. Ross turned around to find the police chief and the district attorney standing a few feet away. *This can't be good.*

"Ross, join us in the conference room," the chief called. "We need to talk." He turned to lead the way. "Have a seat."

"I think I'd rather stand, sir."

"Suit yourself." The chief sat beside the district attorney. "By now you know that Avante made bail."

"Yes. What I want to know is how did he manage to get released? He should still be in a cell."

"That's still being investigated," the district attorney said.

Vagueness seemed to be the flavor of the day, which wasn't going to fly.

"Anyone ask the damn judge?" Ross shot back.

The chief drifted his gaze down, leaving the district attorney to answer.

"We found Judge Watkins' body roughly thirty minutes after Avante walked out of court."

"Money?"

"No," the chief replied. "The entire Watkins family is dead. We found his wife and son's bodies in the basement of their house. So I'm thinking blackmail. We're trying to track Avante down, but he's disappeared."

Alarm bells clanged in Ross's head as his heart tried to beat out of his chest.

"My family."

Avante had sworn to kill everyone Ross loved, for putting him behind bars. His niece and sister were in danger.

"I have to go make sure they're safe."

"We sent a uniform out to watch over your house," the chief said as if it were the solution to everything. "They're safe."

"One officer will not stop Avante and his men," Ross shouted, and flung open the door and ran to the stairs.

His team was hot on his heels.

If one hair on his family's head was touched, there would be nowhere Avante could hide from the hell Ross would rain down.

***

James pulled up behind a black and white, making him wonder if Ross's Crown Vic gave up the ghost and that he had to take a marked cop car home. He still couldn't believe he was here in the first place, outside Ross's house in Pasadena. Ironically, not too far from Finn's and Miguel's home.

After a long dressing, his brother and the rest of the Gates pseudo-family delivered with what appeared to be relish, an order to apologize to Ross for having to put up with his shit. Normally James would've told them to go screw themselves, but Finn had a direct line to James's heart. When the dude got all misty-eyed, James would agree to anything his brother wanted. The little-shit knew how to play him.

So now James sat outside a modest stucco bungalow, without a clue of how to apologize. Hell, he never asked Ross to get involved in his life. The stubborn man did it all on his own. How was James supposed to say he was sorry for that? *Hey Ross, sorry you decided to get involved in my life. I don't think so.*

He let out a deep breath and opened the car door. He might as well get this over with. James noticed all the drapes in the front of the house were closed, but found it odd because it was not even six in the evening. As James approached the cruiser, he glanced inside and found it empty other than a walkie-talkie sitting on the passenger seat.

Since he was young, he always seemed to be able to sense danger coming. His unit called him their lucky charm. Except for that last time. However, if his senses were on the mark, there was much more going on here then he could see.

Instead of walking up to the front door, he decided to have a look around first. He damn-well knew he was paranoid. Hell, if you weren't a bit paranoid while waiting for the next attack, that got you killed fast in the desert. The two side windows had their curtains drawn as well, but he didn't chance it and crawled underneath them so he wouldn't create a shadow. As he skulked in the shadows, he wondered how ticked-off Ross was going to be that James was sneaking around his property.

When he rounded the back, his senses were on alert. Skills he had honed over the years kicked in at the sight of a black Hummer parked on the street directly behind the house. Ross didn't strike James as a man who would pay for an oversized gas-guzzler. From here, it seemed empty, and he slid past the patio door and up to the open side door. After a scan of the kitchen to make sure no one was in there, he crouched down beside the door and listened.

It didn't take long to confirm his suspicions. He wished he had been wrong.

"Take them out to the truck while I leave the good detective a note. Ross will regret the day he heard the Avante name. When I'm done with him, he'll be begging me for mercy."

"Yes, boss," a gruff voice replied, before a woman hissed in pain. "You're coming with us, bitch. You give me any shit and I'll put a bullet in your little girl's head."

"Don't you touch her, you bastard," the woman said. "My brother is going to rip you apart."

James shook his head. Definitely Ross's sister. She sounded as stubborn as her brother.

As the sound of footsteps neared the kitchen, James pulled back around the side of the back deck and waited.

Light footsteps sounded first, followed by heavier boots on the decking. James watched until the woman carrying a young child passed his hiding spot, and then he inched around the corner. The second those boots hit the grass, James attacked quickly and quietly as he could, not wanting to alert anyone still inside the house. The lackey had no idea what hit him as he crumpled unconscious to the ground.

The woman turned, and James put up his hands to show her he wasn't a threat.

"I'm a friend of Ross's." Well, maybe friend was pushing it a little, but at this point he was banking on it being enough for her to trust him.

When she nodded, James lowered his arms and asked quietly, "How many men still inside?"

"Two," she whispered, assessing him with her bright blue eyes.

The little girl shook in her mother's arms, and he was reminded of his younger brothers and sisters. All of them gone now except for Finn.

"Plus they tied up the officer in the back bedroom."

"You need to go hide at a neighbors' and call the police." James instructed as he bent down to pick up the Smith and Wesson the asshole had trained on the woman and her child.

He held it out to her. "Do you know how to use this?"

"Yes," she answered before took it from him.

The way she gripped the handle with ease confirmed she knew what she was doing. He liked this small woman more and more.

"Go," James ordered, and turned back to the house.

Whoever was trying to kidnap Ross's family was still in there. No way was that bastard going to escape while James had the drop on him.

Bringing up all his training, he moved quietly across the deck and into the kitchen. He grabbed two knives from the butcher block on the counter, and readied himself for battle. His mind cleared and focused on the situation before him. The bandages on his left hand would be a hindrance, but he could compensate for that.

"We gonna shoot that cop before we leave?" a deep, scratchy voice asked.

"Yeah. Need to make sure the message to Ross is clear. Clean sweep tonight so we have nothing to worry about."

That had to be the man in charge.

Time had run out. James needed to move before they killed the cop. He flattened his back against the wall between the kitchen and living room. There was a toy dump truck on the floor a few feet in front of him. That would do nicely. He stretched out his left leg and gave the toy a nudge. Sure enough, it rumbled across the kitchen floor and into the other room.

"What the hell is that?" the lackey asked.

"Go see where it came from." The man James figured was the leader spoke with authority.

Perfect. James brought both knives up and squared his stance. He needed to be quick and accurate so that the guy did not get off a shot. As the footsteps came closer, calm focus washed over James. This was the world he knew how to function in.

"It's probably Vince fucking with us," the lackey said, as the barrel of his gun cleared the doorway. "He can be a real asshole."

James attacked with precision, slitting the guy's throat, then grabbing him, silently easing the dead weight onto the floor. As James began to straighten, something flickered to his left. In a blink, he was back in a small village near Kandahar, looking at a mother clinging to her child, her eyes wide with fear as James straightened from his crouch after wiping his bloodied knife on the jeans of the young man he'd killed. Now, as he had then, he blinked rapidly. Then to assuage the censor he felt emanating off the woman: now to clear his fucked-up brain and put his mind back in the room before he became the next victim.

Regaining his focus, he slid the gun from the dead man's hand, then stuffed the pistol in his waistband, at his back. Bending, he made his way behind the sofa, listening to assess the other guy's whereabouts.

Footfall came toward James's position and he rounded the arm of the sofa, keeping low but ready to move.

"Reg?" the leader called. "Where the fuck are you?"

James peered over the arm and saw a stocky guy, mid-forties, surveying the room. When he turned his back, James made his move, charging toward the man whose back was turned. Before James reached him, the guy pivoted swiftly and lunged forward with a large serrated hunting knife aimed at James's abdomen. He sucked in a breath and as he bent his body back to avoid the arc of the swing, he crashed into the coffee table, glasses breaking and crunching under his boots. Losing solid footing for a moment gave his opponent the chance he needed, and the guy lunged.

Sharpened steel cut through James's jacket and shirt, leaving a gash across his right pec. He ignored the pain and moved forward. They swiped at each other, circling. James stayed on the guy, keeping his distance, yet moving in a tighter circle. Reaching for the gun would take precious seconds away from the dance, and he didn't want to throw off his rhythm. He preferred hand-to-hand anyway. Combat shouldn't be impersonal. Taking a life was one of the two most intimate things a person could do. Warriors should be able to look each other in the eye as they advanced their cause.

Moments before James was within striking distance, wouldn't you fucking know it, his foot slipped on the toy dump truck he'd pushed into the room earlier. His balance faltered, and those few missteps was the opening that asshole needed. As James righted himself, he scanned the room and looked through to the kitchen. The patio door was ajar, swinging back and forth from the reverb of having been thrown open.

Shit. The bastard had fled.

James raced out the patio door and saw no sign of the black truck. Shit. He had gotten away.

"Los Angeles Police Department. Drop your weapons and raise your hands over your head, then drop to your knees," a voice ordered, from directly behind him.

James threw the knives out in front of him, then slowly reached behind his back to pull the gun from his waistband before tossing it several feet away. Then he raised his arms and lowered himself to the ground. Immediately, a knee was pressed against his back and his face was buried in the grass. The click of the cuffs echoed in his head as he fought to remain calm. Being incapacitated exacerbated his demons. He may joke about bondage, but this was far from that game.

Shoes appeared in his limited line of sight. Then he was hoisted to his feet and led to the back of the nearest cruiser. He squeezed his body into the backseat, scraping his injured pec against the ridges of the hard plastic seat. All hope of warding off a migraine was lost. He had been getting them regularly since his return to the States.

Another lasting gift from his time overseas.

***

Time crawled as James struggled to hold his shit together. His wounds were beginning to throb, keeping a steady beat in time with his monster headache. More cars arrived, but he remained focused on the glass partition separating him from the front seat. There was a shoe-shaped scuffmark left from what he guessed was some asshole stuck back here who didn't like the accommodations.

He ran maneuvers repeatedly in his head to keep his mind from fixating on his defenseless position. By now, he had cleaned his M16 dozens of times to help keep himself sane. If he ever was sane to begin with.

The backdoor was yanked open, but he refused to turn away from the scuffmark. He had to maintain his concentration or he would snap.

"James."

Ross's voice should've been comforting, but James was too close to the edge.

"Let's get you out of here." Ross reached under James's arm and helped him stand from the vehicle.

James continued to stare straight ahead. He was still a prisoner, at least until someone unlocked his cuffs.

The moment he was free, he paced straight to the backyard. He needed space to breathe and center himself. The culmination of fighting for his life while trying to prevent a mom and child from getting hurt, coupled with his subsequent detainment, were riding him hard. Adrenaline pumped hard through his veins, and once again he had nowhere to vent it.

He tried to block out the chaos around him, and gulped down air as if he were drowning. He heard a single set of footsteps coming up behind him, but at least whoever it was had the sense to stay a few feet back. He was still on the defense and didn't know how he would react to anyone approaching him for whatever reason.

"James, please come with me," Ross entreated. "I have somewhere quiet for you."

James turned around as the detective walked away. He followed him toward the two-door garage behind the house. Ross went in the side door, and James followed behind him. A couple feet in they entered a man cave. A couch, chairs, and a TV graced the area, along with a bar.

"Sit down and relax here until you're ready."

He had no idea how Ross knew what James needed, but grateful, he sat in the quiet, dim room and murmured, "Thank you."

"You got that the wrong way around, buddy." Ross told him as he retrieved a bottle of water from the bar fridge and handed it over.

James couldn't help the hiss when he raised his right arm.

"Are you hurt?

"It's not bad."

"Let me be the judge of that."

Ross moved James's jacket and shirt aside to reveal one of the new gashes that would add one more scar to his war-hardened body. Bullet wounds on his leg, shrapnel tore up his right thigh, and a multitude of cuts and burns made for a gruesome roadmap of war.

The feel of Ross's fingers gliding over James's skin brought an unexpected calm to the roiling anxiety he was experiencing. When Ross pressed his palm against James's chest to examine the wound, James almost moaned. He pulled his shirt back over his wounds, forcing Ross to remove his hand.

"I got distracted. It's my own fault."

Ross looked at him as if he had grown a second head. "You need an EMT to look at that. Are you injured anywhere else?"

"No, not yet. Give it a few minutes and shit might change."

Ross shook his head.

"For real, man. Step away. I need some space."

Ross didn't look happy but he agreed and left. Once James was alone, he coaxed his body to shake off the adrenalin and fear. Being locked in that police cruiser almost did his head in. A head that was still pounding, and the ache shooting bursts of light behind his eyes. While his wounds had stopped bleeding, his state of mind was far from copasetic. His reaction to Ross's touch puzzled him. In the throes of, or even after an episode, and he had been riding the knife's edge the minute the cops cuffed him. He couldn't stand anyone's hands on him. Hell, he couldn't stand to have anyone near him. Yet Ross's warm hands and gentle contact had brought James a relief he'd never experienced. Ever.

He couldn't dwell on that now, and pushed those thoughts aside to examine later. Instead, he needed some intel to make sense out of what'd happened to Ross's family. Why someone would try to kidnap them? He wondered if it had anything to do with the call from earlier today.

Clearly, they needed protection. The venom he'd heard in the voice of that bastard who'd escaped told James that piece of shit would be back. His plans had been thwarted and he had it in for Ross.

Fuck.

James laid his head against the couch and closed his eyes.

He was getting too old for this shit.

CHAPTER 3

Ross was at a loss to explain how he felt. Terror, rage, relief, and something he hadn't felt in a long time, yearning. Touching James had changed something in him, and Ross was not entirely sure he liked it. However, all that didn't matter now, protecting his sister and niece were his top priority.

When he had arrived on the scene he feared the worse, but a scan of the area showed him his family was safe and sound. Jacquelyn and his five-year-old niece, Becca, were standing twenty feet away, talking to an officer. Ross couldn't help himself. When he saw they were safe, he ran to them and lifted them into his arms while apologizing over and over. He shouldn't've ever taken on Avante, knowing the bastard would do anything to put Ross's family at risk.

Of course, Jac was quick to assure him that it wasn't his fault, but Ross knew better. The surprise of the evening came when Jac explained that James had been the man who'd saved them. What had he been doing here? Ross would find out later what brought James to the house, but for now all he could focus on was the release in his chest that his family was safe and that the big oaf had shown up and saved them. The letter Avante left for Ross on the coffee table spelled out clearly that no one he loved was safe or would be as long as Avante drew breath.

Jac and Becca were all Ross had left, and he would pull the sun from the sky before he let anything happen to them.

Several police cruisers were leaving to join the hunt for the lunatic out to destroy him and his family. The officer assigned to look after Ross's house had a concussion, but, fortunately, nothing worse. Ross knew Avante despised the police and took every opportunity to thin their numbers. No doubt, James was responsible for saving the officer's life as well as Ross's family's.

The deck creaked as he walked across it and into the kitchen where his sister was busy cleaning up the debris from what looked like one hell of a fight. Ross could see Becca curled into herself, sound asleep on the couch in the living room. There was still blood on the tiled floor and he knew some of it had leaked out of James.

Why would he risk his life for my family?

"How is the guy who saved us?" Jac asked while dropping Becca's broken dump truck in the garbage.

"James is a little freaked out and is injured."

"Freaked out about saving us?"

"No, I don't think so. I believe it has more to do with being handcuffed and placed in the back of a police car."

"I tried to tell the officers he wasn't one of the bad guys, but they told me they wanted to wait until you got here." Jac explained while picking up what was left of a wooden chair next to the kitchen island.

"Yeah, protocol. Detain everyone on-scene until their identities can be confirmed. I heard they weren't sure how the big guy was going to react if they uncuffed him, since he was trying to melt the center plexiglass with his death stare." Ross couldn't help but smile.

His comment also brought a smile to his sister's face. "I know that they needed to secure the area for their own safety and ours," Jac agreed, but they had to know he was one of them or something like it. Christ, the way he took down that guy leading us to the truck, there's no way he's not trained."

Hearing Jac speak about being led to Avante's truck had the muscle in Ross's jaw jumping as he clenched and unclenched his fists. When he found that piece of shit, someone better be with him or there was no way he would be able to hold himself back from delivering a personal message with his fists.

"He's Finn's brother. Retired Army."

"The one you keep bitching about that you have to look out for? The one you said is irresponsible and thoughtless?" Her look of disbelief was hard to miss.

"Yep, that would be me." James cut into their conversation before he spun around and headed back out of the kitchen.

Shit. Ross hurried to keep up as James passed the last remaining EMT on his way to his car.

"You need to have that cut looked at, man," Ross said.

"I'll take care of it." he answered while opening the car door and got in. "Not your problem."

"We still have to get your statement."

Ross had no idea why he was coming up with excuses to make James stay, when he should've been apologizing.

"Send somebody to the Gates. Not you. Anyone else." Without another word, James started his car and backed out of the driveway, never once looking back.

"I'm an asshole," Ross whispered as the tail-lights vanished around the corner.

***

With his wounds still throbbing, James made his way back to his temporary home. Had he been such an asshole all this time? Was that the way people saw him? He may've gotten himself into trouble a time or two, but he' had always had good intentions even if the results didn't always turn out the way he'd wanted them to go.

He thought about the jerk that had caused him to get stitches earlier today. The asshole slapped a woman. No way would James let that stand. Afterward, the same woman jumped on his back and tried to strangle him, cussin' him out like he'd done her wrong. Talk about no good deed goes unpunished. Then to learn that Ross believed he was thoughtless, reckless, and a pain in the ass, and had no problem sharing that love with his family—James had had enough.

He knew he should've left town after ensuring Finn was safe. Still could. James wasn't sure what was holding him here. He had a head full of memories to deal with, and he knew he was better off being alone. It never dawned on him to call his brother when he took a couple days' drive to clear his mind. He never meant to cause anyone to worry about him. He was so used to living inside his head, and had been without a family for so long, only having a commanding officer to answer to for over a decade the only constraint on his life. When he was on a mission, he understood the objectives and his role within his team. Executing and returning whole were his only priorities for too long and had left him with the kind of memories horror films were made of. To say his interpersonal skillset was limited was so much of an understatement it wasn't funny.

It'd hurt to hear Ross's sister recount his opinion of him. Sure, Ross had said that shit before, but usually when he was yelling at James after he'd done something the po-po didn't like. At the time he'd thought, *too fuckin' bad*. Now? Well, if he was that big an asshole, no one would miss him. Finn was fine. Set up with his man, and they were happy. Mission accomplished. Time to move on.

Having made up his mind his ass was out of here at first light, James needed to get back to his room, take a shower, and assess his physical damage, tend to his wounds, and then pack. He didn't have much, and what he did have would fit in his Army-issued duffle. He liked to travel light.

The one nagging thing James couldn't shake was the need to protect Ross's sister and her kid, but he assured himself that Ross and the LAPD were capable of doing that, especially since they knew the risk assessment had changed.

By the time he pulled into the back parking lot of the Gates, it was nearly midnight. It had been a long day and he hoped everyone else was already asleep. Now wasn't the time for another of their well-intended lectures.

He climbed the back stairs, but it felt more like climbing a mountain. He was bone-tired but still had lots to do. He punched in the code, stepped through and waited for the steel backdoor to relock before heading for his bedroom. As fate would have it, that would be harder than he'd thought.

The hub was…well, a hub of activity. Max, Saint, and Miguel sat on the two couches while Finn stood waiting at the entrance with a large first aid kit in his hands. Goddammit. Ross had called ahead.

"Don't be mad," Finn said. "He wanted to make sure you're okay."

"I'm fine. Going to take a shower and get some rest." He wasn't going to discuss leaving with them. He would leave a note and call Finn from the road. He'd had it with the drama. Like now, everyone in the room wore the same expression, mirroring Finn's concern. Enough.

"If it'll make you feel better," James told Finn, "I'll take the kit and bandage myself up."

Finn gave him a half-smile. His brother knew that was as close to getting medical attention as this was going to get. He handed James the kit and he turned to continue on to his room.

Fuck. Guilt ate at him, so he turned in the hallway to look back at everyone.

"I'm sorry I've been such an ass."

He carried on to his room without waiting for a response.

James closed his bedroom door, dropped the first aid kit on his bed, and headed to the attached bathroom. God, he needed a hot shower. Without fanfare, he began stripping as he walked across the wood floor, leaving a trail of bloody clothes in his wake. He would pick them up later, when he had more energy. The adrenaline crash was bearing down on him, making his muscles twinge and contract. His head spun and he felt exhaustion seep into his marrow.

He didn't even turn on the bathroom light, preferring to leave the door open and let the indirect light serve. He glanced at himself in the mirror as he walked by. Yep, he looked like roadkill. Not bothering to stop to get a better look at his new wound or the dried blood covering his body, he walked into the shower.

Within seconds, he stood under the hot water spraying out of the oversized showerhead, and let it beat down on his neck and shoulders, moaning in pain as he tried to reach for his shampoo bottle. With the cut on the right side of his chest and the stitches on his left hand, every small move caused pain. As he always did, he shoved it down and washed himself. He watched the water turn red as the evidence of today's events flowed down the drain.

He didn't know how long he'd been standing under there, and usually he wouldn't care, but he still had to pack his stuff. He dragged his tired, sore body out of the steamy shower stall. As he dried himself off, he wondered where and when his next shower would be. There was a hint of blood on the towel, which forced him to finally stop what he was doing and deal with his injury.

The bathroom mirror kept fogging up no matter how many times he rubbed it with his towel. Too much work. He walked into his bedroom to get a better look in the full-length mirror on the wall. When he finally examined the cut, he had to admit, he might need stitches. The wound had begun bleeding again, but it wasn't too heavy. He could deal with this. Hell, he'd put himself back together many times. There wasn't always a med unit available when they were in-country, so he and his team had learned to take care of the little shit themselves.

While he stood there examining the most recent slashes in his flesh, he couldn't help but notice the other wounds on his body. Everything from shrapnel caused by an IED in his thigh, bullet holes in various locations from enemy fire, to burns he'd sustained while pulling his combat brother out from their blown-up Stryker. It was a roadmap of war. Every one told a different story and location. He didn't need mementos or pictures of his time spent in the service, he needed only a mirror.

"Oh, my God." Finn gasped, from behind him.

Shit. James hadn't remembered to lock the door. No one had ever seen his scars, outside of medical staff and his unit. Every hookup he'd had since returning had been in dark rooms, or the simple matter of undoing his zipper. The only visible scar was the one that ran down the side of his face, which was enough to communicate his state of being.

"Finn, leave." James didn't need anyone's pity, especially his brother's

"No. You always take care of everything. This time, I'm here to take care of you."

"I don't need to be taken care of." James argued, but it appeared his brother wasn't in the mood to listen as he began removing items from the large medical kit James had left on the bed. "Where the hell did you buy that thing?" It looked better stocked than the ones he'd taken into the field.

Finn hesitated for a moment before saying, "Ross got it for me. You never know what kind of accidents can happen in a restaurant, not to mention the construction zone upstairs."

"Of course."

James should've known Mr. Responsible would have something to do with it being here.

He threw his wet towel on the end of his bed and searched for his shorts. He didn't bother covering up since Finn had already gotten an eyeful. As he pulled on his bottoms, there was a knock on his door.

"What the hell?" James grumbled. Was he having a party?

"Don't worry about it," Finn assured. "I'll see what they want."

While his brother went to the door, James grabbed his canvas duffle bag and set it on the only chair in the room. He needed this night to end and was in serious need of rest, but he had things to finish before giving in to sleep.

Finn came back in and shut the door behind him. Thankfully, he was alone. James raised a questioning brow at his brother.

"It was Miguel checking in to see if we needed anything. He said he'd go out and pick it up for us." Finn looked hopeful.

"Whiskey."

He needed something to ease the pain before Finn began poking around in his wound.

"Got it," Miguel's muffled voice called from the other side of the door.

His willingness to help further solidified that James had to leave. Not good for anyone to be around him, especially these generous people.

"Lay down and let me have a look at your chest." Finn ordered while putting on a pair of latex gloves.

"When did you get first aid training?" James asked as he did what Finn had told him.

"Miguel taught me." Finn answered with a wide smile. "He's an amazing teacher."

"Right, the jarhead," James jibed, trying to dispel some of the tension in the room.

"That's right, grunt." Miguel replied as he walked in with a bottle of whiskey and two glasses.

James had given up trying for privacy around here. At this point, what was another pair of eyes?

"Here." Miguel held out a half-full glass. "Drink up before Finn goes in for a look around."

"My thoughts exactly." James agreed before drawing down on the whiskey.

It still amazed him how his little brother had grown up since James had been out of the country. No thanks to him. That guilt was tacked onto the myriad of others.

"Ouch," James growled. "I wasn't ready."

Finn removed the saline soaked gauze from his chest and grinned.

"You did that on purpose, you little shit."

"Well, you should've let the EMT look at it." Finn continued without missing a beat.

James held out the glass and Miguel obliged. After a couple of deep gulps, warmth spread down his throat and into his belly. That's better.

"You planning on going somewhere?" Miguel asked as he removed the duffle from the chair and sat down with his own glass.

What was the use in lying? "Yeah. Thought I'd hit the open road for a while."

"You're leaving?" Finn's voice deepened.

"For a little while. I'll come back and visit. It's time for me to go find my place in this world." If that was even possible. "Okay, I'm ready. Dig away."

Finn looked like he was about to argue, but with a shake of Miguel's head, he stopped himself. James appreciated it. He didn't have the energy to defend his decision to leave. He took another drink from his glass before laying his head back.

"So where've you been stationed?" Miguel asked, probably in hopes of distracting him.

"From the Sangin District of Helmand Province in Afghanistan, to Somalia and all the hot spots in between. Or at least that's what it felt like." James muttered while trying to clear his mind of what Finn was doing. "Different stations, same old, same old." He emptied his glass and held it out for a refill.

As Miguel refilled the glass, Finn finished with his *examination*.

"I think I can glue this chest wound shut. It's a clean slice."

"Here, here, for Ross having quality kitchen knives." James raised his whiskey in salute before tipping it back.

He was feeling the whiskey faster than usual. He hadn't eaten anything other than that damn lollipop, and couldn't find the energy to care if he sounded like a frat boy.

"You know you're a hero, right?" Finn asked.

"Hero… shmero. I was in the right place at the right time. Nothing more."

He didn't want anyone to buy into that hero shit. In the military, he'd seen real heroes, and as with most of his teammates, not one of them felt that way about themselves. They'd had a job to do and they did it. They moved on to the next mission and did what they had to do.

It seemed Finn wanted to argue the point but he refrained. That worked for James. He wanted to float away into sweet oblivion, on an amber river.

Fuck Ross. Why does it still bother me so much to have heard Ross's sentiments coming out of his sister's mouth?

"Maybe because they hurt you," Finn answered.

"Shit, I'm not drunk enough to have said that out loud."

"Oh, yeah you are," Finn assured with a smile as he held the wound closed, allowing the skin glue to set.

A few butterfly bandages and a covering of gauze and James was all patched up Again.

"Now take it easy for a couple days or that might split back open. You're already on a round of antibiotics and your tetanus shot was updated this morning."

"Yes doctor," James deadpanned.

Finn shook his head. "Now let's check out those other cuts and the stitches on your hand."

James shifted to grab his whiskey with his right hand and promptly hissed in pain from the move. He set the glass down on his bed since it was empty anyway and presented Finn with his left hand. After another thorough cleaning and re-bandaging, he was about ready to crash.

"We'll talk in the morning." Miguel left with the bottle of whiskey.

Damn.

Finn packed up the first aid kit and brought the covers up over James. "Love you, big brother."

James was struck with concern. "You know I love you, right?" James never thought to ask. He had been away a long time.

Finn stopped in the doorway and looked back at him with a big smile. "I've always known that."

The light went out and his door shut. Finally, he was alone.

CHAPTER 4

The next morning, James slept in later than he had wanted, but was up and ready to go in no time. One of the many benefits of not having much by way of personal belongings, he travelled light and fast. He was surprised no one had knocked on his door by now. He took a final look around before leaving his room and walking down the hall.

When he turned the corner into a now crowded hub, he knew why they hadn't bothered him. The usual crew had added two new arrivals, both strangers and definitely cops. They turned to look at him when he entered. At least Ross was nowhere to be found.

"'Morning. You hungry?" Finn asked from the small kitchenette. "I have bacon."

"Nice try. What's going on?" James asked, even though he was considering the bacon.

A woman with pitch-black hair introduced herself. "Mr. Masterson, my name is Beverly Hines and I'm a detective with the LAPD."

She didn't bother to introduce the guy standing beside her.

"You've come to take my statement? That's good, because I was getting ready to head out." The quicker he got this over with, the quicker he could put LA behind him. His brother was safe and loved, it was more then he'd had hoped for. So it was time for him to go."

"I'm Detective Sparks, and I'm sorry to inform you but you can't leave the city," the man beside Beverly said, though he didn't look sorry. "You're a material witness to a crime and we need to take you into protective custody."

"No shittin' way." James set his bag down on the concrete floor. "I'll give you my statement and sign it. You need me to come back for trial, I'll come."

"A contract has been taken out on you. Avante wants you dead." Beverly explained.

James looked around the room at the shocked faces. "Why does he want to kill me? How does he even know who I am?"

"You've cost him his chance at getting at Ross's family. Now we're prepared for him," Sparks answered. "As for how he knows your identity," the cop shrugged, "we're still looking into that."

"How can you be sure Avante took out a contract on my brother?" Finn asked as he came over to stand next to James. "Maybe it's someone else."

James didn't like to the look on his brother's face. This was bullshit.

Beverly's face lost some of its steel before she answered Finn. "We have CI's all over the city that keep us up to date on this type of activity. It's been confirmed."

"I'm gonna refuse protective custody. I'm good at taking care of myself."

James told the cops. They knew he wouldn't be easy to take down, and if he left, he'd draw attention away from his brother and the Gates's crew.

"You can't," Finn exclaimed as he grabbed James's arm. "I can live with you not staying in LA, but I won't lose you now that I just got you back."

Ah shit. His brother's pleading gaze drained the fight right out of his body. James couldn't say no to Finn, even after all these years. James remembered how he had hid Finn multiple times when they were younger, which meant harsh punishment, but he'd never cared. Finn was his brother and James would die for him.

Fuck.

So much for his escape from Los Angeles.

"When do we leave?"

***

Ross heard the vehicle pull in, and moved the heavy curtain a sliver to get a look at who was coming up the path. He didn't know why he bothered checking. Bev had already texted him that they were on their way back with James.

"Standing there looking pissed off is no way to welcome our new housemate." Jac said as she entered the living room of their safe house.

"I'm not angry. I'm concerned." Ross muttered as Becca ran over to him with "uppie" hands.

He lifted his niece and cuddled her in his arms. The backdoor opened and he watched Bev walk in through the kitchen, followed by James and Sparks. The moment James laid eyes on Ross, his expression changed from annoyed to flat-out anger.

"What the hell is Ross doing here?" James asked Bev as if Ross wasn't in the room.

Jac came over to collect her daughter and took Becca down the hall.

"I'm here to protect my family until Avante is caught," Ross growled.

"I'm out." James said before turning around and heading for the door.

"You promised your brother," Bev was quick to point out. "By having the four of you in one place, it'll make it easier to defend. We won't have to split up our manpower."

"Wrong." James punched his finger at Bev. "I have more experience than the lot of you, and putting everyone together is a clusterfuck."

"We know what we're doing." Sparks waved off his concerns, making James double down.

"Do you? Do you really? Then tell me how having everyone Avante wants dead in one house is a good idea for anyone other than Avante. It'd certainly make his job easier."

"We have officers stationed around the property and patrolling the roads in this area. You're completely safe," Sparks stated.

"I don't know if you're being intentionally dense or if it's a natural occurrence, but this is not safe. I've spent years protecting civilians. My team and I kept people safe in war zones. Trust me, all of us in this house is *not* safe. Fuck, man, the place might as well have a bullseye on its roof."

"We aren't in a theater of war. This is our domain and we know what we're doing. This is the correct protocol to keep everyone safe from Avante," Sparks argued.

"When will this bullshit stop? When will you people learn and listen to me?"

Sparks shook his head and strode out the room, muttering.

James sighed and his shoulders dropped. "Haven't I paid enough for one lifetime?"

Ross knew it was a rhetorical question but couldn't remain silent. "I'm sorry I hurt you."

James spun so fast his duffle almost fell off his shoulder. "Hurt me? You don't have that kind of power, Detective. Where do I bunk?"

"Upstairs, last door on the right," Bev answered.

With one final glare, James was up the stairs as if the fires of hell were on his heels.

"Well, that went well." Jac remarked as she reentered the room. "That has to be one of the lamest apologies I've ever heard. *Sorry I hurt you*. Come on."

"What?" Ross asked.

It was a damn apology. What the hell else was he supposed to say.

"For the love of God. How about, thank you for saving my sister and niece, and sorry I'm such a tight ass." Bev offered, making Jac laugh.

"Fuck all of you." Ross returned to the paper-strewn dining table. "There are more important things to worry about at the moment."

"Where's Becca?" Sparks asked.

***

James threw his duffle on the bed and sat down on a nearby chair that groaned under his weight. Why had he agreed to this? He buried his face in the palms of his hands and saw Finn's face. That's why. Moments later, he heard his door opening. James was ready to rip a piece off Ross if he had followed him up to his room.

He looked up, ready to let Ross have it, and quickly changed his expression from anger to confusion. Ross's niece walked in and came over to him with her hands up. Anyone knows what an uppie looked like, so James obliged and sat her on his knee.

"Hey, darlin', what's your name?" James asked the adorable blue-eyed little girl smiling at him.

"Becca."

"Well, nice to see you again Becca. I'm James. How did you get up here?"

"The stairs," Becca answered as if that should be obvious.

"By yourself?"

"Yeah."

"How old are you?"

"Five," she said while she shoved her chubby fingers in the air counting five. "Are you mad?"

"Nope."

Memories of his sisters and brothers washed through him. Being the oldest meant a lot of responsibility. He'd clean up after them, do their laundry, cook their meals, all while his parents sat in church to hear the Founder drone on and on about the coming of the end of the world. He missed his siblings every day, but at least he still had Finn.

"Maybe we should go let your mommy know where you are, sweetie. She might worry."

"Okay."

As James stood up from the chair, with Becca in his arms, his bedroom door opened wider, revealing Becca's mother and Ross.

"I'm sorry if she was bugging you," the woman said as she walked in to take Becca. "My name is Jac, short for Jacqueline."

Before James had a chance to let the tot go, Becca wrapped her arms around his neck and hugged him. He couldn't help but smile.

"Nice to meet you, ma'am. Becca wasn't a problem. Got a lot of sibs." James shifted the little girl into her mom's arms.

"How many brothers and sisters do you have?" Jac asked, which made Ross cough.

"I only have one now, ma'am. Finn." A sad truth.

He could see the realization dawn. Did everyone in Ross's family have blue eyes and black hair?

"Oh, I'm so sorry. I didn't mean to pry. I didn't know." Jac was quick to say as her free arm zigzagged through the air.

James placed his palm on Jac's waving hand. "It's okay, ma'am. No harm done. I don't mind talking about them. It helps with missing them so much."

He should've stayed behind to care for them instead of joining the army. He might've been able to save them. However, with his father's ultimatum, James had had no other choice. Either he left, or he would've had to marry a girl from a neighboring family.

Jac composed herself, and before James knew what was happening he was back in another hug. Other than Finn, he couldn't remember the last time he had been hugged so much. He looked up to find Ross staring at them closely. When he saw James watching him, Ross quickly looked away.

Jac straightened and tugged on the small apron she was wearing that proclaimed her *The Best,* in sparkles.

"Supper will be at six," she told him. "I expect to see you at the dinner table."

"Yes, ma'am."

"And stop with that ma'am shit. I'm not that old."

"Mommy said a bad word." Becca said while pointing to her mother's face.

Jac's cheeks got red.

"I'm sorry, baby. Mommy shouldn't have said that. It was wrong of me." Jac hugged her daughter close and turned to leave. Then she reached out and punched her brother in the arm. "That's how you apologize."

James blinked and stared at his boots to keep from laughing.

Moments later, she was gone, leaving Ross and James alone. Instead of following his sister out, Ross sat in one of the room's chairs.

"Oookay," James mumbled, as he went to his bag, and began unpacking.

He wasn't in the mood for another discussion with Ross.

"Bev and Sparks weren't gone long. You must've packed quickly."

"Nope, I was already packed."

"Where were you going?"

"Anywhere other than LA."

"What about Finn?"

"Miguel is taking good care of him. I'll come back and visit."

Ross went silent, and James continued pulling shit out of his bag. At this rate, he was going to be out of stuff before the guy left. James slowed it down.

"Look, James—"

"No," James growled as he turned to look at Ross. "I get it. We don't need to rehash shit. You don't like me. I'm good with that. Now if you don't mind, I'd like to clean up before supper."

Jac would prefer it, and considering she was such a kind woman, he would oblige. The fact that she'd punched Ross didn't hurt either.

Ross sat staring at him for a few more moments before finally standing up. "If that's what you want."

"Yes, Detective, that's what I want." James bit out every word to make his point.

He didn't need to stand there listening to a list of his faults. He thought those days were behind him when he left the cult. It was one thing for Ross to say it to James's face. A completely different thing when it was behind his back.

Ross nodded and walked out, closing the door behind him, which should've given James some relief, but it didn't. He couldn't get the feeling he'd had at Ross's touch, out of his mind. For whatever the reason, the cop calmed him in a way no one else ever had. Which didn't make a fuckload of sense since all they did was argue. And clearly, Ross didn't hold a high opinion of him.

With everything that was in him, for all the obvious reasons and the hidden ones, James hoped they'd find Avante fuckin' fast before the situation in this house became as dangerous to James's health as the threat Avante and his minions posed.

CHAPTER 5

Ross sat alone, staring at the files surrounding him. "Where are you hiding?"

Someone had to be helping Avante stay this far beneath the radar. This was the third day of being confined in a safe house and he was going stir crazy. It didn't help that James had avoided him like the plague. It surprised Ross how much he missed their usual banter. The man had been a pain in his ass from day one, and he didn't listen to a word Ross said. He'd have to be crazy to miss that shit, but dammit he did.

As if James meant to rub it in, he was friendly and helpful to Jac and Becca, playing on the living room floor with the little girl more than once. Infuriatingly, Ross found himself more distracted by what James with doing than working on finding Avante. True, it wasn't his case to work on, but with his history with Avante, he had a lot to offer the team… if he could only focus.

Ross looked up to see James dressed in only his jeans, leaning against the doorway, the wound on his chest a reminder of what the man had done for him and his family. That red mark was the least of his scars. His body a road map of sacrifice for his country.

"You know it's two in the morning?"

Ross wasn't sure if he was more shocked by James's appearance so late at night or that he was talking to him after three days of silence. "Lots of things to take care of."

"Like what? Maybe I can help." James offered.

Okay, Ross knew he hadn't fallen asleep, because his arm burned where he was currently pinching it, so he wasn't dreaming this.

"A fresh pair of eyes wouldn't hurt." Ross would accept any help offered to find Avante.

"I'll take that as you meaning to say, 'James, thank you. I would appreciate your help.' But I'm not going to split hairs." The bastard grinned.

Ross pinched himself even harder.

"What's going on?" Cause sure as shit, this was not happening. "You haven't talked to me in days. Now you are here offering to help. What gives?"

James took a few more steps into the room and said, "I want to call a truce."

"A truce?"

Ross was leery. It seemed too easy.

"Yeah. While we're hiding out. There's a lot of tension between us and I don't want it to affect Becca or Jac." James appeared to be genuine, but even as Ross acknowledged how well James had been treating Jac and Becca, he was still wary.

"I agree. We need to work together to protect my family." Ross could not help but thaw a little knowing James cared for Becca and Jac.

"I will protect them with my life," James said, with vehemence, and Ross believed him.

"You already have. Thank you." There was nothing else he could say. His gratitude was all he had at the moment.

James came over and took a seat in the chair across from Ross. He picked up the file closest to him.

"Maybe it's best if I get a feel for this Avante, from the beginning."

Ross leaned over, grabbed a two-inch thick folder and handed it to James.

"These are all my notes. I have spent years building a case against the POS. He never liked to do his own dirty work, so gathering intel meant I had to get creative."

James stared at him closely. Ross was not sure what he was looking for. "This is personal."

"Yeah. He's after my sister and niece." Ross stated the obvious.

"No, I mean before Avante tried to take them. There's more to it." James narrowed his eyes as if he was trying to peer inside Ross's head.

Scary thought, nobody in their right mind wanted to see that.

Ross didn't know how James had figured that out so quickly, but there was no use keeping it a secret.

"Avante is responsible for my brother-in-law's death."

"Becca's father? Jac's husband?" James confirmed.

"Right. Mark got himself into a world of trouble."

"Money? Drugs?"

"Gambling. By the time Jac found out, it was already too late. Mark had remortgaged their home, sold all the jewelry our mother had left Jac, and he'd burned through their savings and Becca's college fund. Then he started to borrow money from the wrong people."

It still burned him that Mark hadn't come to him before destroying Jac and Becca's lives.

"Shit. He borrowed from a loan shark?"

"Worse. He made a deal with the devil, by the name Avante. If Mark didn't repay what he owed within sixty days, Jac and Becca belonged to Avante."

Even saying the words made Ross sick.

James stood so fast his chair fell over behind him. "The bastard wanted them for…"

"Yeah. Sick fuck. Thankfully, Mark had a shred of decency left. He didn't have the money, but at the sixty-day mark he went to the meet location but didn't bring Jac and Becca. A week later, his body was found in the gutter, near San Pedro. It appeared he'd been kept alive for days while Avante *questioned* him."

"So you made it your mission to put Avante behind bars." James shook his head, his brows drawn together, low over his eyes.

"Yeah. I had to make sure he never came after Jac and Becca, and I had to take that sick fuck off the streets for good."

James righted his chair and sat back down. "Okay. Let me read through this file tonight to get up to speed." He suddenly averted his eyes and twisted the paper in his hands. "Did that piece of shit mean to pimp out Jac and Becca?"

"Human trafficking is my best guess, but I'm not sure. Avante is so twisted, who knows what's in his head" It didn't matter what Avante intended to do with Jac and Becca, the only thing that mattered was making sure he never got the chance to try. Mark owed over two hundred thousand dollars. Avante wanted his money back and would take it by any means necessary."

James's lipped thinned and set his jaw. "Saint told me about something like this happening to friends of his brother, Johnny. They brought in some specialists to help."

"We have cruisers in the area and officers around the property. We're alert and we're not where Avante expects us to be."

"Really? Have you figured out how Avante found out who I was so quickly?" James asked pointedly but didn't wait for a reply. "I know you have faith in the LAPD, but I'm just sayin', this guy is motivated. Think on bringing in other people." James waved the folder and then stood.

"James, we're safe here," Ross stated.

"Keep telling yourself that." James turned on his heels and went upstairs.

Ross knew James had seen and done a lot in various conflicts around the world, but Ross knew LA and his fellow officers.

"My family will be safe," Ross whispered, and for a split second, he wondered whom he was trying to convince.

Damn it, James.

***

He felt like he had been run over by a truck, and was in desperate need of caffeine. After returning to his room and reading through the file, there was no way in hell James could've fallen asleep. Avante was a cruel and sadistic bastard, and imagining Jac and Becca being anywhere near him, filled James with rage. Avante had been implicated in so many criminal activities, most of which prayed on the innocent. Prostitution, human trafficking, drugs, and gun running. Anyone in his way moved or disappeared.

After showering and getting dressed, James made his way downstairs, He carried his boots. He didn't want to wake anyone else since it was well before six in the morning. His need for coffee had him heading straight for the kitchen. The house was quiet and it seemed as if he were the only one up. He peeked through a curtain to see the officers were spread out around the property. He figured they'd be in for coffee soon and decided to brew a full pot.

He leaned against the counter and waited, then heard a muffled voice outside the kitchen window. He leaned over the sink to listen in on the conversation.

"Yes," a voice said, and James recognized it as Sparks. "I've taken care of it." Then there was a pause before Sparks continued.

"Has the money been deposited into my account?" Another pause. "Yes. You have a thirty-minute window. Make it count."

Fuck. Sparks had sold them out. James grabbed the only set of keys from the hook and rushed back upstairs to Ross's bedroom. The second he opened the door, Ross sprang from the bed, his gun drawn and trained on James.

"Stand down, man."

"What the hell are you doing?" Ross growled, as he wiped the sleep from his eyes.

"We have to go. Avante is on his way." Time was of the essence. They could not stay here and shoot it out until help arrived.

Ross glared, but James could see the fast pumping blood in Ross's neck.

"How do you know? The officers are—"

"Not going to be of help. I overheard Sparks making the arrangements. We have to get the girls out of here."

Ross looked unsure for a moment.

"You have to trust me to protect your family. Now, Ross. We're running out of time."

Ross looked him in the eyes for a beat before finally nodding and reaching for his pants. James hightailed it to Jac and Becca's room and hoped neither one of them screamed at having him walk in there. Thankfully, Jac was already awake and sitting up in bed with Becca still asleep beside her.

"What's wrong?" she asked.

"We need to go. Avante is coming. Get dressed, but stay in here and take only what you need. Ross or I will come get you."

Without any further questions, Jac reached for Becca to wake her. James left them and ran for his own room. He grabbed his duffle from the top shelf of the closet and threw what was necessary in it, then unzipped the inside pocket he had added to the bag years ago, and reached in and pulled out his Glock, along with three clips. He shoved the clips into his pockets, checked the safety, and tucked the gun into the back waistband of his jeans. With one final scan of the room and a quick text to an old Army buddy, he was ready.

By the time James made it into the hallway, Ross and the girls were waiting for him.

"I'll head down first to make sure it's clear." James threw his bag over his shoulder and onto his back, then pulled out his gun before heading down the stairs.

Every creak seemed amplified as he honed in on their surroundings. When he made it to the bottom, he placed his bag on the floor and pressed his back against the wall between the living room and kitchen. James let out a breath, brought his gun up at the ready, and then stepped around the wall and into the kitchen.

The house was as empty as it had been when he'd first come down to get caffeine. The smell of coffee teased as he went to the kitchen window once again and gently pushed the curtain back enough to see the front yard. Sparks stood about twenty feet away in the middle of the driveway, undoubtedly waiting for Avante and his men to show up. Fleetingly, James wondered how much money it took to buy off Detective Sparks.

When James got the chance, he'd educate the detective on the error of his ways. For now, he had to get everyone out of there.

He walked back to the bottom of the stairs and waved to Ross, whose gun was drawn. Jac carried a sleepy Becca, who was held close to her mother's chest.

Ross checked the back of the house while James stayed up front.

"My car is about ten feet from the backdoor," Ross whispered.

James reached into his pocket and pulled out the keys. "These for it?"

"Yeah."

The dude was cool under pressure. James would give him that.

As James turned from the window, the sound of tires rolling over gravel alerted them to imminent danger. He took a second look to confirm it was indeed Avante and his men, almost hoping he had been wrong. The same black Hummer that had been sitting at Ross's house pulled to a stop beside Sparks, and a tall Asian man got out of the passenger seat. The file James had read last night had an assortment of pictures of Avante in it, and there was no mistaking this was the asshole from the fight.

James didn't have to say a word. Ross was already leading his family out the backdoor. James grabbed his bag off the floor and followed them out. Ross scanned the area while James covered their backs.

A few feet away, they found the first officer face down in the grass. Ross leaned over to check for a pulse and shook his head. James didn't expect anyone was meant to survive today. As if to confirm it, in the distance a second body lay motionless against the tall wooden fence running along the west side of the property.

Sparks would pay. James would make sure of it.

He positioned himself in front of the car as Jac and Becca climbed in the back. Once they were in, James made his way to the driver's door, never taking his eyes or his gun off the house. Avante's men should be coming around the back to surround the house anytime now. James glanced over to find Ross trained on the house as well, only on the passenger side of the car instead.

With another nod, both got in the car.

"All hell is going break loose when I start this car."

"I'll be ready," Ross answered, and James had no doubt. He had seen the same look in the eyes of the men in his unit. Nothing was getting past Ross.

James put the key in the ignition and turned over the engine. At least the car was pointed to the back alleyway. The moment he dropped the car into gear, he floored it and skidded out into the alley, taking a few trashcans with him.

"Get down," Ross yelled, seconds before bullets ricocheted off the car.

Jac and Becca's heads disappeared, and James figured they were lying on the floorboards. Their screams tore a hole in his heart, but it was the safest place for them.

In the rearview mirror, James watched several men running out into the alleyway as he picked up speed. Avante and his men weren't even trying to hide their guns, completely unconcerned if they hit an innocent bystander. Fuckin' pieces of shit.

James knew they would be in their vehicles, racing after them in moments. He had to figure out how to lose them and fast.

"Stay down for now, Jac." Ross ordered as he turned back around in the passenger seat to face forward.

"I have a plan," James said. "I need you to get us out of the city." He hadn't been in LA long enough to know how to stay off the radar. He needed side streets and fast.

"Which direction?" Ross asked, without even questioning to find out what the plan was.

James would take that as a win. Ross trusted him. For now, anyway.

"South."

"Turn left at the next intersection," Ross directed. "Hand me your phones."

Jac's shaky hand came up over the front seat and she dropped her phone beside her brother. James pulled his out and did the same.

"Before you destroy them, maybe you should send your chief a message to let them know what's going on," James suggested. "Sparks killed those officers."

"Already on it, I'm also sending a copy through the precinct message board. Sparks won't be able to hide," Ross promised. "He'll pay for what he's done."

James turned the corner as instructed, while the noise of crushing glass told him that Ross was destroying each phone before throwing them out the window.

"We'll need a different car. This one is traceable." James thought about getting his own vehicle, but Avante would already know which was his.

"Turn right into this alley." Ross pointed at a small alley between two rundown apartment buildings.

"Why can't we go to the station?" Jac asked, from her hiding spot.

"Sorry, sis, we don't know who else might be involved. It's too big a risk," Ross explained.

Jac then asked, "Can you hand me my purse? I brought toys for Becca and animal crackers."

The little girl was so quiet James wondered how much of this situation a five year-old would understand. He prayed this wouldn't scar her for life.

"Turn right and then left," Ross instructed. "We'll stop and switch out cars before we get too far out of the city."

"Who are we switching with? Are they trustworthy?"

"Yeah. I've known Bev for over twenty years."

"Won't that be one of the first places they'll look?"

"At her home, sure, but we aren't going there," Ross assured.

James could see the pain of betrayal in the detective's eyes and didn't bother to ask, knowing Ross needed a few minutes to wrap his mind around everything that'd happened.

After it settled, it would simmer, then burn in his gut. There was no help for that. Even making sure Sparks got what was coming to him wouldn't bring back all the officers he killed today.

CHAPTER 6

They'd lost Avante and his minions about five minutes out of the city. Years of trolling every nook and cranny of LA and its environs had given Ross the edge they'd needed. For now, they were safe to find another vehicle and get on the road to execute James's plan.

Ross scanned the winding road, manicured yards, and sprawling estates before opening his car door.

"I won't be long."

James nodded, never taking his eyes off their surroundings. Ross knew to his core: his sister and niece were safe with James.

Jac and Becca were now sitting up in the backseat. The anger radiating off Jac was only tempered when she glanced down at her daughter. Ross felt her fury and was certain it was amplified by the betrayal of a brother in blue. He had known Sparks since the guy joined their team four years earlier. Everything Sparks had done since day one was suspect. Every arrest they had made, every case they'd closed would be under scrutiny. Hundreds of criminals behind bars would be tagging their attorneys to file motions to get them out of jail. Fuckin' Sparks. Had he been working for Avante the entire time?

Now wasn't the time to analyze and dissect. There'd be time for that later. Ross had to get another vehicle and fast.

He walked up to the side door of a house he couldn't afford in his wildest imagination. The electric bill would've been as much as a sensible mortgage payment. He pushed the doorbell and waited. He'd be lying if he said he wasn't nervous about asking for help, but at this point, he had no one else to trust and he didn't want to bring the Gates crew into this.

A tall man with salt and pepper hair, wearing a dark navy suit answered the door. "Mr. Mayor, I'm sorry to disturb you, but I need to speak with Bev."

"How many times have I told you to call me John, outside of city hall?" Mayor Weere asked while glancing at the car Ross had arrived in. "Come in."

John held the door open for Ross as he walked into the spacious kitchen.

"I'll go let Bev know you're here."

As the mayor was about to leave, Bev came racing into the kitchen, almost taking the swinging door off its hinges.

She held her cell phone in her hand and said without looking up, "Babe, I've gotta go, Ross is in danger." Bev looked up and took a stuttered step back. "Ross, what the hell is going on? I just read your message."

"I don't have time to explain. I need to borrow a car. Sparks is working with Avante, and if it wasn't for James my family would be as dead as the officers we found around the safe house."

"Shit. You can have mine," Bev offered.

"I don't know how many people are involved, but at this point you're the only one I can trust," Ross explained.

"When I find Sparks, I'll squeeze that information out of him," Bev said as she grabbed her keys off the kitchen island. "What else do you need me to do?"

"Try to find out how far this goes. That's the only way we'll be able to stop Avante."

Until now, the Mayor had remained silent. "They'll be able to trace your car, knowing that Ross would come to you. Take one of mine instead. No one will be looking for it."

"Good idea, babe," Bev agreed as she went to a small cupboard beside the door and pulled out a couple sets of keys.

Since Bev and John's relationship wasn't public knowledge, Avante wouldn't think to look for one of the mayor's vehicles. Clearly, Avante had his snitches in the department, but few people knew about her and John. Understandably, Bev wasn't ready to deal with the media frenzy that would come with being the detective who was dating the mayor.

"Give him the keys to the Tahoe. It has more room, tinted windows," John suggested.

Bev rifled through the keys and came up with the set for the Tahoe. "Here." She stuck out her hand to Ross.

He took the keys and said, "I'll get James to move my car around back so no one will see it from the road. Thanks for this."

The two men shook.

"I've destroyed our phones. I'll reach out to you from a burner," Ross said.

"Understood." Bev nodded. "I'll figure this out on my end. You and your family need to stay safe until we have Avante and all those involved locked up."

"Thanks, Bev." Ross hugged his friend before walking out the side door.

He motioned for James to drive the car up the driveway as he walked to the back of the mansion. The four garage doors were sliding open as James parked in an empty space inside the right bay.

Ross went to his car and grabbed his bag out of the passenger seat before opening the backdoor. "We have a new ride."

James looked around before resting his gaze on Ross. "Never figured you ran with the upper crust."

"I don't," Ross replied. "But friends do come handy in a pinch."

He helped his sister from the backseat, while James lifted Becca into his arms before grabbing his own bag. Quickly, they loaded themselves into the black Tahoe.

"It's going to be all right, Jac, I promise." It struck him that he'd said the same thing to James last night. He hadn't taken James's concerns seriously, and now look where they were.

"Between having you and James, I might actually believe that, bro," Jac said, from the backseat.

James stood inside the opposite backdoor, sliding the seatbelt around Becca. They didn't have her booster so that was going to have to do for now.

Becca held on tight to her stuffed toy puppy and James's arm.

Gently, he unattached himself and leaned down to look Becca in the eyes. "I promise to protect you and your mommy. Don't be afraid."

"Like before, at home?" Becca asked, in a small voice.

"Yep, Just like that."

Becca smiled for the first time today and lifted her puppy up. "And Puppy, too?"

"Of course. We can't let anything happen to Puppy," James answered before kissing Becca on the top of her head and shutting the door.

***

James climbed into the driver's seat and Ross didn't say a word. James figured Ross knew it was best to keep moving allowing the person with the plan to take the lead. Unless something happened to James, Ross would remain as the designated lookout.

The safest place James could think of, on a moment's notice, was owned by a volatile veteran who'd been on James's team. He hoped Jack had calmed a bit over the last five years since he'd been honorably discharged. This could blow up in their faces real quick if Jack hadn't settled.

The engine roared to life and James pulled out of the garage. The woman he had met before, Bev, stood on the back deck with a tall older man.

"Is that the damn mayor?" James asked.

He had seen the guy's picture in the newspaper.

"Yeah. But that stays between us." Ross nodded at Bev.

"Fair enough. As long as you trust him." At this point they couldn't be too cautious. They'd already trusted one rat.

"Bev does, and that works for me."

James slowly drove down the driveway. It would look suspicious if he sped out of the estate. Everything needed to appear as normal as possible until they cleared the gated community. He headed towards the I-5, obeying every traffic law and the speed limit, even if it pissed off the other motorists.

"There's a small television on the back of each of your seats," Jac remarked. "There's even remote controls."

"See if you can find anything for Becca to watch.," Ross suggested before he turned his question to James. "Where are we headed?"

"To a friend's."

"And where is that exactly?" Ross asked as upbeat music from a cartoon began playing in the back.

"A former teammate. Jack's a private man. His place is off grid. It's at least a couple hours from here. You need to trust me, Ross."

"We'll need to get food soon for the girls."

Without any further inquiry, Ross confirmed that he trusted him, and James didn't know why he felt so gratified about that fact.

"Since we'll be on the five for a while, you'll need to stop at a gas station that has food to hold us over."

"Gotcha. We have a good hour on here."

"Okay." Ross replied as he pulled out a paper map from the glove box.

"They actually still make those?" James asked.

Ross shook his head and began unfolding the map.

They stopped once to pick up some food and two burner phones, where Becca and Jac used the restroom. James grabbed a phone for himself, knowing Finn would've found out what'd happened by now, and was likely upset. James would call his brother the moment he had a chance.

"You know the phone numbers from your old phone?" Ross asked as he began setting them up.

"I only had four phone numbers on it, so I'm good," James explained.

"Only four? Now I have to know. Finn, obviously. Miguel, and maybe this Jack guy."

James nodded as Ross named them off. It was not like some big secret or anything.

"Saint must be the fourth."

"Nope. That would be you, Detective."

"Me?"

"Don't look so surprised. It's not as if I just proposed. It was only a number. Hell, you were always around anyway, so I really didn't need it." James had no idea why he was getting so defensive.

Ross had a strange look on his face. "I'm glad you included me among the four."

James didn't bother answering and decided to concentrate on the road ahead. They'd exited the freeway a while back, and were now making their way up a winding road, heading east into the mountains. This wasn't the time or place to be getting any notions of hooking up. Shit, he didn't even know if Ross was gay. Probably best to leave well enough alone. But when had James ever done that?

Another hour went by before James began seeing subtle signs that they were getting closer to Jack's property. A black ribbon tied around a tree, an old shirt left dangling from a wire, and finally, the row of granite rocks weighing at least a ton each, blocking the goat path they had turned onto.

"Doesn't look like your friend wants visitors," Jac said from the backseat. "Are you sure about this?"

Becca had fallen asleep about twenty minutes ago, which was fortunate considering the welcome they were sure to receive.

"I wouldn't have brought you here if I thought any of you would get hurt."

James backed up the SUV and set the four-wheel drive. He didn't fool himself into thinking that Jack didn't already know they were there. He was probably watching them through a scope right now. The engine revved as James carefully made his way around the roadblock and up the pitted trail. Surprisingly, it appeared that the rest of the path had been cleared.

Several minutes later, he pulled the truck to a stop outside a steel shed set against a steep incline, its large garage door slowly rising. He could feel the tension in the truck skyrocket when he began driving into the shed.

"Take your hand off your gun for the next few minutes, man."

Ross nodded and did as asked.

The door slid shut behind them, plunging them into darkness. Only the vehicle's running lights provided illumination. Everything remained quiet as James searched for any sign of Jack among the oil drums and crates.

Sure enough, a small red dot blazed on James's chest. Ross reached for his gun.

"No, take it easy or you're going to get one of us hurt. I'll deal with this." James lowered his window and yelled, "Rocketman, I have a woman and child in here so put that shit away."

"Like that'll help," Ross muttered.

The lights turned on.

"Yep." James nodded. "It did."

A rope dropped from above in front of the truck, and they watched as Jack, in black fatigues, his long red hair tied at the nape of his neck, climbed down from his perch, his rifle tied to his back.

"Seriously," Ross said.

"Safest place you'll ever be, besides with me."

James assured without breaking eye contact with Ross, willing the detective to believe him even though his buddy had repelled from the rafters like some hopped-up GI Joe.

When Ross didn't argue, James took it as another good sign and reached for the door handle. Jack waited until James stepped out to approach the vehicle. When he did, Jack took a long look inside.

"You sure about this, man?" Jack asked.

"If they couldn't be trusted, I wouldn't have brought them here." It seemed both sides of this equation had the same thoughts.

Jack stared him dead in the eye. "On your life?"

"At the moment, my life is already on the line."

James was pulled into a back-thumping hug by his wired-for-sound teammate. Jack may've looked rough around the edges, but he was harmless. Or at least sane enough to know the difference between friend and foe.

"It's good to see you, buddy. What've you been up to, other than pissing off crime bosses?" Jack asked.

"How'd ya know?"

He sure hadn't put that in the text.

"Wallflower's been taking a poke around in the police department's servers since you told me you were coming."

James should've known. Wallflower, aka Wendy, would have been busy checking out the police chatter, the Internet, and the dark web.

"The police servers?" Ross asked as he joined them in front of the truck.

"Detective Ross," Jack greeted. "Don't worry, we never do anything illegal. But having intel is a must around here."

"And what is *around here*?"

"You didn't tell them?" Jack asked.

James shook his head. No need to explain. Ross would find out soon enough.

"Well then, welcome to our little community of preppers," Jack said. "El Hogar. We've been preparing for the end of our civilization for over fifteen years."

CHAPTER 7

What the hell have I gotten us into? Ross scanned the area that Jack had led them to with his truck, which had been hidden behind the shed. Small wind turbines and solar panels covered every roof in the community of ten large prefabricated houses. True, he trusted James, but he wasn't the man Ross was worried about.

Each house looked similar to the others. The only difference he could see was the paint colors. They varied between sandy brown to light green, and blended in well with their surroundings. For obvious reasons.

Ross looked over at Jac to find her staring at the other Jack's ass. "For God's sake, this isn't a social visit. Don't get any ideas."

"Sorry, bro, but ideas are abounding." Jac said as she waved her hands in the air.

"Shit."

Ross looked up at James, who was carrying Becca in his arms. She was still fast asleep. The kid could sleep through a tornado. Becca was becoming attached to James and Ross worried what would happen when all this was over. Before James had been forced into the safe house, he'd intended on heading out of town for parts unknown.

Jack continued to point out various things as they walked in-between the houses. He seemed proud of what they'd built, and Ross couldn't fault him on that. They appeared to be completely self-sufficient. Members of the community began coming out of their houses and following their little group, until they reached the front of one of the houses painted green. They followed their host up the steps to the front porch. When they were at the top, Jack turned around to address the other members of the community.

"My friends, these are the people I've told you were coming. An evil man responsible for terrorizing them has gone as far as trying to kidnap this mother and child. You all know who James is, from previous visits, and this man is Detective Ross. His sister and niece were targeted. There's no doubt in my mind that this Avante will try to kill all four."

Ross felt the sting of those words straight to his heart. He'd do anything in his power to keep Jac and Becca from being hurt, even if he died ensuring that.

"Like to see him try to get past us," a man with a lengthy handlebar mustache called out.

"That's right," an older woman with greying hair agreed. "We've prepared for this eventuality. We're ready for whatever this joker sends our way."

Ross watched as more than thirty people began agreeing, making plans, and setting up watch schedules. He looked over at James, who was grinning.

"Safest place you could be."

Well, damn. James had been right.

***

James laid Becca on the soft bed in the guestroom where Jac and Becca would be staying. The room was plain but had everything they needed. A dresser, bed, lights, and surprisingly, a TV. That was new. He wondered how they were getting reception, considering they wouldn't allow the satellite guy to come moseying in to set up a connection.

When he stood back up, Jac wrapped her arms around him as far as she could reach.

"Thank you for all this."

Before James had a chance to respond, she released him.

"Now go out there and come up with a plan to stop Avante. Between you and my brother, you'll figure it out. You two make a good team."

James wasn't sure what to say about that, so he said nothing and simply nodded before leaving the room. Team, yeah, right: a police detective and the man responsible for the deaths of his unit. There would be no team. James never wanted to be a part of one ever again.

"What's got you so worried," Ross asked, as James entered the kitchen.

"Nothing," James replied.

The last thing he wanted to do was rehash that memory, and sure as fuck he had no intention of sharing it with Ross. Bad enough James had to carry that shit around in his head. No way was he "sharing," especially for reasons he had no desire to explore. He didn't want Ross to think worse of him than he already did.

Ross didn't seem to be buying it, but the squeal coming from the porch, quickly followed by a young woman running through the door took everyone's attention.

"You're back," she cried, as she jumped into James's arms wrapping her legs around his waist. "Finally. It took you long enough."

James glanced over to see Ross studying the situation, and Wallflower noticed as well. Nothing got past her.

She jumped down and said, "I'm sorry. I'm only his friend. Are the two of you together?"

Ross looked at James before saying, "We're friends."

"Why? He's prime. Aren't you gay?"

Leave it a twenty year-old to stab right at the heart of the matter.

"James is gay. You know that, right."

"It's never come up," Ross replied without answering the question directed at him.

"So?" Wallflower wouldn't let it go until she got an answer.

"Wallflower, now is not the time," James admonished.

"Yeah. I'm gay."

Wallflower brightened and said, "Perfect." She eyed them. "You look good together."

James shook his head in an attempt to clue this wild child to get herself under control. Of course, she didn't pay attention.

"You two will be sharing a bedroom. We're all full up. Maybe you guys can explore the possibilities later."

If James could've thought of any way out of this situation, he would've taken it, but he was speechless. Shot through the heart by a short, wafer-thin technical genius.

"Wallflower, that's enough." Jack said as he set three coffees on the kitchen table. "You stay out of your uncle's love life."

"But don't you see how they look at each other?" she argued, waving her hand between Ross and James.

What? James looked at everyone the same way. Or at least, he thought he did.

More shocking than the implication of the statement was Ross appeared unfazed by the conversation. He sat back in his chair with his cup of coffee and seemed to be getting great joy out of seeing James squirm.

"Not going to help?" James asked.

"No, I'm good." Ross answered flashing that cat-had-a-saucer-of-milk grin he wore when he was getting his way.

"I like him already." Wallflower announced as she removed her messenger bag from over her shoulder and pulled out her laptop.

They may've been survivalists, but to them technology was yet another tool to ensure their continued safety.

"Got something for you to look at." She opened her laptop, hit a few keys, and turned it so James, Ross, and Jack could see the screen.

"What are we looking at?" James asked. Other than numbers, he had no idea what he was seeing.

"These are Avante's bank records," Wallflower said without any apparent concern she'd hacked into a mobster's accounts. "Don't worry. I've rerouted this sucker so many times that it would take a wizard with a golden ring to find me."

James looked at the numbers more critically this time. At first, he couldn't believe what he was seeing. This couldn't be correct.

"Is this everything?" he asked.

"Yes. Every penny." Wallflower looked proud of herself.

James had to hand it to her. She was a prodigy.

Ross asked the question that was on James's mind. "Avante's broke?"

"Yep. All his accounts now have negative balances."

"He's been cut off," Ross stated.

"Cut off?" James had no idea what that meant for a mobster.

Ross couldn't hide his shock. "I've always suspected that Avante had someone to answer to. Now I'm sure of it. Is there another name on those accounts?"

"Why, yes, Detective, there is. But I ran B. Gen's name, and I wasn't able to find anything under that alias."

"You can't track them down?" James was surprised.

Wallflower had never come up against something she couldn't unravel.

"I'm not done with this. I'll find out who this is." Wallflower assured.

"So, this B. Gen took the money?" James asked for clarification.

"That's what appears to have happened," Wallflower confirmed.

"When was it drained?" Ross asked.

"Seven this morning. Coincidently, the same time news broke about gunfire in an alley in a residential neighborhood north of DTLA."

James watched the lines between Ross's eyes get deeper as he concentrated on the screen. If anyone could figure this out it would be him.

"He didn't kill us," Ross said as if that were news to James.

"Yep, and I'm happy about that," James said. "Your point?"

"No, whoever this B. Gen is, he cleaned Avante out when he failed to kill us. He's been disavowed by the family." Ross went on to explain, "When Avante lost us, the higher-ups cut him loose. He's now become a liability."

"Does that mean he won't be able to come after us?" James asked.

"I'm not sure. Until he's back behind bars, there's no guarantee he won't do it to make a point."

"The police are searching for him. Avante won't be free too much longer," Jack said before taking a sip of his coffee.

James reached for his and downed half the cup in one gulp. For obvious reasons, he hadn't had a cup of the coffee he'd brewed that morning.

"Wallflower, lunch is ready," a teenaged girl named Rainbow hollered, as she walked through the door.

Rainbow and Wallflower were sisters.

"I'm off. Lots to do," Wallflower said before pointing between him and Ross. "Now you two play nice, unless you want to get kinky, then go for it."

Once Wallflower got something in her head, she was unstoppable. He was prepared to suffer a long couple of days of ribbing.

CHAPTER 8

His hands shook as he clenched his jaw even harder. How could they do this to him? He had been loyal, done whatever was asked of him. *Now they act as if they don't even know me.*

"Another drink, boss?"

Avante looked up at one of his faithful crew who had stuck around even after everything he'd worked so hard for was taken away. He couldn't remember the guy's name, and never cared to learn it along with the other ten of them, but since he held out a bottle of whiskey, Avante acted like the guy mattered.

"Fill it up," he slurred. *How many have I had?*

Whatever the number was, it still wasn't enough to dull the betrayal.

Once his glass was full, the other man left to join the others. Avante didn't share his room with anybody. They could all bunk in the next room. He wanted to be left alone so he could think of a way out of this.

Over twenty years of taking all the bullshit, back-stabbing, and hits taken at him, only to be hung out to dry. He had worked his way up from being a street dealer to having his own crew. Years of scrounging for his share of the pie had been washed away in a matter of minutes. No warning or second chance.

"To hell with that," Avante bellowed, but his men knew better than to answer him. He was close to losing his shit, and no one wanted to be in the line of fire. He'd had prestige and power. Gorgeous women threw themselves at him, and nobody dared to tell him no.

Gone, all of it.

All because one cop got all bent out of shape when Avante killed his low-life brother-in-law. By rights, the wife and daughter were his, as the debt remained unpaid. The asshole had begged to leave his family alone, but a contract had been agreed upon. Honestly, he didn't care how, but he would get his money back, one way or another. The lives of two people meant nothing to him unless they proved useful.

Avante looked around the dingy motel room. Vinyl drapes covered in green and yellow flowers, cockroaches lying dead on the floor, a bed that looked ready to collapse, and strange noises bubbling up in the toilet. This was what he had been reduced to. His downtown condominium, his cars, his suits, his money, everything was taken from him. *Fucking Bastards.*

The room reminded him of the life he had grown up in. His mother was a prostitute, and his father a drug dealer. He had spent his childhood living in motels, barely able to go to school and always hungry. His clothes had holes and his shoes were always either too big or too small, depending on what Goodwill had available.

His mother brought home men, even with Avante and his dad there. How fucked up to allow a child to watch his mother having sex with different men almost every night. No wonder he was quick to pledge his loyalty to the first group who offered him a job as a runner when he was fourteen. After he was "jumped in," Avante had never looked back from that day, until now.

No matter how bad things looked, he'd sworn this was far from over. First, he would kill that cop, his family, and the asshole that'd decided to be a hero. Then he'd go after those who took everything away from him and forced him into this hellhole. It was time to clean house. Out with the old and in with the new, leaving Avante on top.

No more rules, answering to anyone, or being told what to do. Those days were over. He would usher in a new era, where everyone who worked for him wasn't afraid of the cops and didn't rely on the "old ways." Where old men sat back, making the decisions and expecting others to follow them. The last time they'd walked the streets, Carter was president. What did they know about the reality of the city when they lived in mansions in gated communities? They were so far away from the reality of getting their hands dirty that they had lost their edge.

Hell, this might've been the kick in the ass Avante needed to bring about this change, and he would take full advantage of it. Now, he needed to find Ross and end this.

"Boss, you're going to want to take this call," Viper, his second-in-command, said as he raced into Avante's room.

"Who are you to decide what I want. Get the hell out." He had plans to make.

"But they say they know where Ross is."

That got Avante's attention as he ripped the cell phone out of Viper's hand. Things were looking up already.

***

Ross stood at the end of the bed and had no clue how this was going to work. He looked over at James, who seemed as uncomfortable as he was.

"I'll sleep on the couch," James said.

"That beat-up old thing, hell no. You need to get decent sleep if we're going to make it out of this. We're adults. We should be able to sleep in that bed together without it being a problem."

Yeah, right. Sleep with a handsome, half-naked man who I've had a hard-on for. Shit. Okay, so maybe James wasn't half-naked. He had sleep pants and a t-shirt on, and he looked damn fine in them.

"Sure, I bunked with my unit." James stopped and got that pained look in his eyes once again.

"Why do you get upset when you talk about them?" Ross asked. It had happened on multiple occasions.

James's head shot up so fast Ross was amazed it didn't go flying off his neck.

"I'm not upset. Now remember, keep your hands to yourself, Detective."

Ross wasn't surprised that James was defensive or that he was trying to steer the conversation away from him and onto their sleeping arrangements. Ross would let it go. If James wanted to tell him, he would.

"No problem. You stay on your side of the bed, I'll stay on mine," Ross shot back.

He knew James was smart enough to realize that Ross was giving him a way out of the conversation and he took it. "That's all worked out. Which side of the bed do you sleep on?"

"Right."

"Good. I like the left side."

Neither moved from the foot of the bed. If anyone saw them, they would laugh their heads off.

Ross gave in and made the first move. He rounded the right side of the bed and pulled the covers back.

"Let's get on with it," Ross said. "I need some sleep."

"Don't sound so excited," James replied before going to the other side of the bed.

Ross could feel the mattress dip when James sat down. He had been sleeping alone for so long that something as simple as the bed shifting felt odd. Ross reached over his night table and turned off his lamp.

"Goodnight."

"Goodnight," James replied before Ross heard the click of James's lamp turning off, blanketing the room into darkness.

At least they couldn't see each other, though Ross was acutely aware of the man less than a foot away.

After a few moments, Ross relaxed. It had been a long day, so he began drifting off to sleep. He would deal with whatever else came their way, in the morning. One night of peace was all he wanted, and thanks to James bringing them there, Ross would have it.

Handsome bastard was never wrong, even when he was doing something wrong.

***

James woke and the first thing he noticed was the muscled arm wrapped around his waist. The second was Ross's warm breath on the back of his neck. Hearing the occasional snore, James was sure Ross was still asleep. What now?

In truth, what was really pissing him off was that he couldn't bring himself to move Ross's arm away. James wasn't a cuddly guy. He didn't snuggle and all that shit. Apparently, that had changed, along with a few other things. Starting with how attached he'd become to Jac and Becca. It was simpler when it was only Finn. Even the big, bad detective had wormed his way in, and James wasn't sure how to get him out. Or if he even wanted to.

He looked at his watch surprised to see it was only three in the morning. Which meant he would likely be in this position for hours if he didn't move. He searched for reasons that it was a bad idea, but came up empty. Confirmation he was fucked.

Decision made, he laid his head back down and simply enjoyed the closeness. He couldn't remember a time he'd been held in comfort when sex wasn't on the table. It never crossed his mind before. He had grown up without any affection from his parents, and believed that was normal.

The next time he woke, the bed was empty. James sat up and looked around, but Ross was gone. He could see the sunlight filtering in around the drapes, so it had to be morning. He couldn't help but wonder if Ross had woken up and bolted when he realized his arm was wrapped around James.

Who cares? Get your head on straight, deal with Avante, and make your break from LA as planned.

He didn't need this complication, and kicked himself for allowing it to happen. He should've moved Ross's arm away the moment he saw it around his waist.

"Good morning," Ross said as he walked into the bedroom, still dressed in his sleeping pants. "I know how much you need coffee when you wake up."

Ross handed James a mug before taking a sip from his own. James didn't know what to say, so he took a gulp of his coffee. The pain was immediate as the hot liquid burned his mouth. Coffee sprayed out of him as quickly as it had gone in.

"Shit, I should've told you it was fresh out of the pot," Ross said as he set down his mug and grabbed a towel from the attached bathroom. "Here, let me see."

James laughed. "You shouldn't have had to warn me. Hell. Coffee is hot."

"Open," Ross instructed as he loomed over James. "Let's see the damage."

He followed instructions as Ross took a look inside.

"Well, you might get small blisters forming on your tongue." Before Ross backed off, he stopped to wipe the remaining coffee off James's chin.

Their eyes locked for a split second, but that was all James needed to see the hunger in Ross's eyes. Acting on instinct, James stood abruptly and backed Ross into the bedroom wall before taking his soft lips in a needy kiss. Ross responded in kind, running his hands over James's back and arms. He tasted of mint and coffee driving James on for a deeper exploration. He could feel Ross's body responding as James rubbed his hard cock against Ross's.

"Oh, crap. I'm so sorry." Jac's voice stopped them and they jumped apart like teenagers caught necking on their parents' couch. "The door was open."

"Uncle James, are you Uncle Ross's boyfriend?" Becca asked as only a child could.

James reached back, grabbed the comforter off the bed, and held it up in front of Ross and himself.

"Um... boyfriend... well..." James had no idea where he was going with this.

Jac took Becca's hand and said, "Honey, we need to leave these two alone so they can continue talking."

Though that smirk on her face meant something else entirely.

Once the girls had left, James looked at Ross and then wrapped his hand around Ross's thick neck. James could see the longing in Ross's eyes even as he moved away.

"Not a good idea."

"You want it as much as I do. Great way to blow off steam after all that's happened."

"No. I do not want to confuse Becca. When you leave, she'll be sad enough. Best to leave it," Ross muttered. He picked up his bag from the chair and walked out of the bedroom without ever looking back.

What the hell just happened?

James threw the comforter back on the bed and headed for the bathroom. Maybe a shower would help, but he doubted it.

Now that he'd had a taste of the sexy detective, he wanted more.

CHAPTER 9

His muscles were aching and his jeans were covered in dirt, but Ross didn't care as long as it got him out of the house and away from James. When Jack suggested building a rock partition around one of the wells, Ross had jumped all over it. He was out the front door before James had even got out of his shower.

It was hard to miss his sister's stare, but he was only thinking of Becca and protecting her. Emotional pain was still pain, no matter how you framed it.

"So, James got you all twisted?" Jack asked as he wiped the sweat off his forehead with his sleeve.

So far, they'd been working in silence, which Ross preferred. Looked like that was over.

"Not twisted. Facing reality," Ross huffed as he lifted another block into place. "How do you know, anyway?"

"Your sister told me." Jack smiled wide as if that were some kind of victory.

"Of course she did."

Ross should've expected that. Once she got something in her head, she was unstoppable.

"What's the problem?" Jack asked. "Winky having a hard time standing at attention? I hear older men—"

"No problems in that area, and I'm only forty-five."

Jack raised his hands in mock surrender before lifting another cinder block onto the wall. Ross was glad the conversation was over. He had enough problems on his radar already. He didn't need a chorus of *why not do James*, coming at him.

"Well, I see it a bit differently. You're afraid," Jack said. His expression of dawning knowledge was comical, as if he'd figured out some great secret. Apparently, Jack wasn't good at hiding his emotions.

"I'm not afraid of James." At least, not physically.

"No, not him. Yourself," Jack explained. "You're afraid to let go of your control over the situation. You need to take the bull in there by the horns and have yourselves a little bedroom rodeo. You know, dancing in the sheets, get your bone honed, and launch the meat missile."

"Ya know, I've been a cop for a long time, and gotta admit, I've never heard it put so colorfully before."

"Maybe. But that's beside the point. When was the last time you got laid?"

"Oh, hell no. Can't we build these damn walls in silence?" How had his sex life become the morning's topic of conversation?

"Okay, okay. If that's what you want." Jack nodded as if he understood.

"It is." Ross wanted to make sure he was clear on the subject.

Without saying a word, Jack returned to the blocks, and peace ensued. Ross would have to have a long chat with his sister. His private life wasn't open to visitors.

"I'm just sayin', you need to take chances. Life is short. Take what you want and to hell with the repercussions." Jack chopped his arms through the air as he spoke.

Ross dropped the block he was holding and walked away. There was no way he was going to get into a conversation about what he should do with his sex life. He would rather face his sister, who true to form, was waiting on the front porch for him.

Slowly, he climbed the stairs, his aching body refusing to move faster. Ross had been at it since first thing this morning, and it was now after lunch. Sure, he'd went to the gym regularly and kept himself in shape, but hauling cinder blocks around for hours was nowhere near what he did at the gym or on the job.

"Don't," he said, as Jac opened her mouth. "The other Jack has already driven me away with his questions. I need a hot shower and maybe an hour or two of sleep."

Ross knew Jac and Becca were safe here. No one was getting within fifty miles of the place without the community knowing about it. He could take a few hours to regroup and rest. When he walked through the door he was greeted by the sight of James lying on his stomach on the living room floor as Becca set out tea for the three of them. Puppy being the third member of the party.

"Uncle Ross, do you want to have tea with us?" Becca asked. It took everything in him to shake his head. He loved playing with his niece. It had always been a highlight of his day.

"I'm sorry honey, but I'm all dirty. I need to take a shower," Ross explained.

"Why are you walking funny?" Becca asked.

"Because Uncle James's friend is insane."

Becca laughed. "You're funny, Uncle Ross."

Ross reached for his bag, which he'd left on the couch, and headed back to his bedroom. His body ached and he needed some peace. He dumped his bag back on the same chair he had last night, and pulled out a pair of old shorts. Some of the seams were fraying, but you didn't throw things away because they were older.

By the time he made it into the shower, all he could manage to do was stand under the hot stream of water. After about ten minutes, he reached for the bar of soap to wash away the remnants of the day. Too bad he couldn't do the same with this morning. He felt like a jerk. James had done exactly what Ross had wanted. Then he'd pushed James away. Talk about mixed signals. Ross wasn't a game-player. He believed in being up front and honest, even when it was difficult.

Exhausted, he turned the knobs and stepped out of the shower.

He had to admit, when he had first heard the word "prepper," he'd imagined outhouses and cooking over a campfire. What did he know? He had never run into a survivalist before. Or at least, not that he knew of.

While the bathroom may not have been fancy, it was tiled and spacious. The house had a fully functioning kitchen, and a washer and dryer.

Ross wrapped the towel around his waist and stepped out into the bedroom to find James sitting on the bed waiting for him.

"Look, James, I don't—"

"Hey, we're cool. I came in to save you from yourself," James said. "How did you ever get talked into helping Jack? The man is a machine. He could go on all day and never get tired."

"Information I wished I'd had earlier."

Would it have changed his decision? Probably not, he'd needed space and the physical exertion. Well, not to that extent, but at the time he'd needed to burn off his frustration.

James waved a tube of something in Ross's direction. He must've looked wary 'cause James laughed.

"Don't worry, man, it's muscle cream to help you relax, or you're going to be in traction for days. You're no use to us if that happens."

Ross hated to admit it, but he felt foolish. Like James would brandish a tube of lube after being cool about Ross bugging out. He reached for the creme only to have it pulled out of his reach.

"I thought you said it was for me."

"It is, but the shape you're in, there's no way you'd be able to do it properly. Lay down on your stomach, I'll take care of it."

Fuck. This was asking for trouble. Did that stop him from lying down? Hell no.

Ross held his towel in place and crawled onto the bed, which took more effort than usual. Once comfortable, he settled onto the soft mattress with a loud groan. What had he done to himself in an attempt to avoid James?

"Yep, trying to keep up with Jack is a mistake," James muttered as Ross heard the cap come off the tube and tensed.

"Easy. Going to work these knots out so you can sleep."

"Why are you being so nice?" Ross had to ask because this was above and beyond.

"Is it so hard to believe I want you to feel better?" James asked sounding a bit insulted.

"When you put it that way, no," Ross acknowledged. James had been helping his family from day one. "Sorry."

"Don't worry about it. Hell, at times I don't even believe myself." James laughed, making Ross smile.

The first touch to Ross's shoulders sent ripples of awareness through his body. When James knelt on the bed to get closer, Ross let out a soft moan.

"Does it hurt here?" James asked as he worked on Ross's shoulder blade.

"Yeah." He couldn't come up with any other reason for the moan, so he went with that.

Ross was having doubts that he'd be able to make it through his massage without doing that again.

"Okay, try to relax. The worst is yet to come."

Ross could hear the smirk in James's voice even though he couldn't see him, and growled in reply, but was soon back to groaning as James worked his way around Ross's body. Those calloused hands were working miracles. Of course, every squeeze was painful, but soon enough, his muscles began to loosen.

Every time James ran his hands over Ross's skin, a rush of desire flooded his body. He could feel his cock growing harder, and Ross was powerless to stop it.

He'd wanted James for a while. Now, even though his first priority was his sister and niece, James was quickly carving out his own spot in Ross's life. How long could he hold out from going after what he really wanted?

His thoughts were interrupted when James said, "All right, turn over."

Shit. "Um… that's not such a good idea at the moment." There would be no way to hide his raging erection.

"Why?" James asked, but Ross had a suspicion that James already knew. "Come on, roll over. I promise not to move the towel, unless it's an emergency."

Ross knew James was joking, but couldn't bring himself to laugh. If he turned over, the hard-on he was sporting would make his towel into a tent. Talk about mixed messages. First, he pushes James away, and now he was in a towel, lying in bed, with a sexy, hot man hovering over him.

"Gotcha," James said. "Don't worry about it. That kind of thing happens all the time, especially while getting a rubdown. Some need no more than a stiff breeze. It's nothing to be ashamed of."

"I'm not ashamed of my dick being hard."

"Then roll over." It sounded so simple when he said it. "If it makes you feel any better, I have one, too."

"Yeah?" *Did that make it better?*

"Yeah. I've got my hands all over you. What'd you expect?" James asked as if that was a given.

"I don't want you to get the wrong idea. What I said this morning still stands."

"Yep. I understand you're concerned about Becca's feelings. I would never intentionally hurt her," James assured.

"I know you wouldn't." Ross sighed. "Fine."

He flipped over, and sure enough, his towel was tented.

James carried on massaging Ross's arms as if rubbing down a man with a dick as hard as steel was an everyday occurrence. Ross had no choice but to close his eyes and relax his head back onto the pillow. James's hands felt so good, and he was skilled. Eventually, even with what was going on under the towel, Ross's muscles relaxed.

By the time James had finished with the massage, Ross felt like his body had sunk an inch deeper into the mattress. His arms and legs seemed so heavy he couldn't move them. His body felt like heaven, except for his throbbing cock begging for release. He'd have to take care of that after James left, or he would never fall asleep.

"Thanks, man. I feel better already."

"Good. Now let's talk about the elephant in the room." James touched Ross's hip. "You're never going to fall asleep until that's taken care of."

Ross's eyes flew open.

"Calm down. I know the score. No one needs to know."

"Why are you doing this?"

Seriously, was James horny and Ross was the only other gay man around?

"Simple. I'm attracted to you. Is that so hard to believe?"

"Going years without even a hook-up tends to alter one's view of himself." *Shit. Did I say that out loud? What's wrong with me?*

"You didn't want to bring anyone home because of Jac and Becca. I understand that. Though, I don't know why you didn't get a hotel room. Whatever. I respect your choice, but it's time for you to take care of you." James pulled off Ross's towel and wrapped his big hand around Ross's straining cock.

Ross couldn't help but moan. It had been too long and he wanted James badly.

"I thought you promised not to remove the towel."

"Only if it wasn't an emergency. This, right here," James said while squeezing the base of Ross's cock, "is an emergency. Lay back and enjoy yourself for once, Detective."

Then without warning, his cock was engulfed inside a warm, wet mouth. James's talented tongue circled the head of Ross's cock before dipping into the slit. He reached for the second pillow to cover his mouth, hoping to drown out his groans of pleasure.

"Damn, Detective, you taste good," James growled as he rolled Ross's balls in one hand while pumping his shaft with the other. "That's it, babe, let go of that control you wrap around you like a wall."

"Oh god, yes."

Ross gave up the pretense that he didn't want this as badly as James did. He spread his legs wide and cocked his knees to give James more room to explore. But Ross didn't fool himself into believing this would be much more than a hook-up while they were here at the compound.

"That's it, open for me," James said, his voice rough and low.

While sucking him down his throat, James slid his hand further down until his finger was circling Ross's hole. Damn, he was so close. He gripped the bedding like a lifeline as he thrust his hips upward and his cock deeper into James's mouth.

James slowed his movements, allowing Ross to take back a bit of control. It was a heady feeling having his sexy soldier take what Ross was giving him and coming back for more. His head was buzzing and he began to feel tingling at the base of his spine.

"I'm going to come," he warned, not wanting to catch James off guard if he wanted to pull away.

Instead, James began pumping his head up and down even faster before he stuck the end of his finger into Ross's hole. That was it. Fire raced up his spine and through his body seconds before he came down James's throat. His body began to spasm as he hollered his release into the pillow.

His ears were ringing as he tried to catch his breath, then it hit him, and he began to explain, "Shit, I'm clean. Really. I have to go get checked regularly for work and insurance. I can show you when we get back home."

James wiped his mouth on the corner of the towel before gently cleaning Ross with it. "I didn't doubt you were. It had been years, and I know you would've stopped me if there was a concern."

"Yeah, man. I would have."

James pulled the covers over him, then placed his hands on either side of Ross's head before kissing him. Ross was on overload as their tongues dueled for control. He felt like he was going under until James pulled away with a satisfied smile on his face.

"Don't worry. I have condoms for the even more pleasurable pursuits to come." James kissed him once again before bringing the covers even higher and saying, "Now go to sleep."

Long after James had left, Ross laid there playing all possible scenarios through his head. From ending this whole thing right now before anyone got hurt, to finding reasons that this arrangement could work out. By the time he was drifting off to sleep, he had decided to take things as they come.

Who knew what tomorrow held.

CHAPTER 10

James zeroed in on his target and squeezed the trigger. The feel of the recoil was as familiar as breathing. The pungent smell of afterburn wafted through the air.

Binoculars stuck to his face, Jack hollered from behind James, "Nice shot. Dead center. You've always had hell of an aim. Made me jealous as fuck."

James secured his gun and stepped away from the firing range Jack had built. "This is nice. When'd you set it up?"

"About two years ago," Jack answered. "Thought it would be important for the community to have a place to practice safely."

"Smart idea."

The last thing they needed was to have guns going off in different trajectories when someone decided to shoot off a round or two. Or when they needed to confront the enemy.

James stretched his knuckles, pulling on the stitches that should be coming out in a couple days. The incident with the pimp seemed so long ago. Almost as if it never happened.

"Thank you," Jack answered with a bow. "Now, let's talk."

"What?"

He should've known something was on Jack's mind. He was a great friend and a combat brother, but he also thought of himself as a bit of a therapist.

"Hey, I'm looking out for you, buddy," Jack said. "Do you really want to hitch your horse to that wagon? After all, it's basically a premade family, and you've always been a lone wolf kinda guy."

James wasn't sure why that statement pissed him off.

"You can keep your damn opinions to yourself." But Jack wasn't the type to listen or be deterred from his path.

"It's not like I'm saying they're not nice people. Hell, they've been friendly, helpful, and respectful of our ways. No doubt about it, that detective is a straight-up kind of guy. I like him. But, man, I've known you forever and you have never done long term. It's like you're skipping a couple steps, going from single without commitments to an uncle, brother-in-law, and partner."

James understood his friend was only watching out for him, but the more Jack made his points, the angrier James became.

"When did you become a relationship coach?"

"Have you seen the folks around here? Didn't tool them up regular…chaos," Jack said by way of an answer. "But you do admit you're in a relationship."

"Seriously, dude. I'm holding a gun."

Jack laughed. The bastard had a death wish.

"Come on, you can't stand there and tell me this is more than a fling. Something to occupy you until Avante is taken out. Plus, the guy's kinda old."

James saw red. Everything inside him wanted to shove those words right back down Jack's throat. Before he consciously thought about it, James closed the distance and got right up in Jack's face.

Nose to nose, he growled, "Don't talk about Ross without respect. He risks his life every day trying to keep that damn city as safe as he can. He takes responsibility for his sister and his niece while hunting down the bastard who killed his brother-in-law. As for Jac and Becca, you won't find a more dedicated mom and sweeter child anywhere. So for the last time, keep your opinions to yourself."

James could hear his blood pulsing in his head as his body coiled to strike. He hadn't been this angry in a long time. Then his asshole friend cracked a huge grin, and James knew he was being played.

"Sorry, man, but I like them and I wanted to make sure you were taking this seriously before you get in too deep," Jack admitted. "They're good people. Arguably better than either of us deserve."

"Either of us?" James asked as he stepped back.

For the first time James could ever remember, Jack blushed.

"Yay, well, Jac is um… nice."

"Nice? Do me a favor and brush up on your elocution before you make your big move, Neanderthal."

James wasn't surprised by Jack's admission. Everyone had to have noticed the two Jacks had been exchanging looks for the past three days. Maybe Jac and Becca might want to stay here after all was said and done.

Jack waved an oily rag in the air as he spoke. "Yeah, yeah, yeah. It's been a while since I had to be all flowery and shit."

"For example, don't say things like that." James laughed, but he was still unsettled about his reaction to what Jack had said about Ross. "I'm going to take a hike and have a look around."

"Take as long as you need, buddy," Jack said as he began dismantling his rifle.

James checked his gun, grabbed a bottle of water, and headed out. A couple hours alone would be good for his head. Things were getting complicated, and he was the last person who needed any more complications in his life.

The mountains were a welcome reprieve from the city. Oaks, maples, and beeches mixed with pines, firs, and spruces kept the forest floor cool and soft to tread. James enjoyed the backcountry, a peaceful place where he could lose himself. Peace didn't find him, though. The longer he walked the more confused he became. The exact opposite of what he had been hoping to find. Why did shit always come at him the hard way?

He crested a small ridge and sat down on a table of rocks. Ross had him so messed up that James had almost knocked out Jack. The moment that thought entered his mind, he felt guilty. That wasn't Ross's fault.

There was something about the detective that drew James to him. He was having a hell of a time fighting it. From his overactive sense of responsibility to his quiet moments when playing with Becca, that family had come to mean something to him in a short period of time. As Jack had said, James had been a "lone wolf" for a long time. Putting down roots had been an anathema until now.

When James saw Ross walk into the house, moving like a stick figure, he'd had the best intentions when he'd offered to massage Ross's sore muscles. Well, maybe the thought of having his hands all over Ross had crossed his mind, but it wasn't until he had laid face down in the bed that James's desire overcame his good sense.

He had felt desperate to hear Ross moan in pleasure instead of pain. What was wrong with him? James had never considered someone else's pleasure without expecting the same in return. Walking away with a steel rod in his pants had been a first.

He wondered if he was doing the right thing for Ross and his family. He wished he knew the answer. He didn't want to be an asshole. Maybe he should stop this before it went any further. That thought turned his stomach. What would be so wrong with enjoying Ross and their time together? As long as all displays of affection were done out of Becca's sightline, there was no reason not to indulge.

Maybe he was overthinking this whole thing. Ross hadn't stopped him or voiced any objections when James had mentioned there would be more to come. They were grown-ass men. Yet James was concerned that he didn't have control over his emotions. Look at how he'd reacted to Jack.

James had locked away his emotions so many years ago, and to say he was out of touch with them was laughable. Before he met Ross and his family, James was all about action and moving on. Now the damned feelings he hoped he'd buried deep seemed to have rushed to the surface at the worst possible time.

James was leaving LA when this was over. He had already made that decision, and Ross knew about that. It wasn't as if James was trying to keep things a secret, or attempting to take advantage of the situation.

He felt off-kilter, which was fucked up. He was always sure of himself, but now he felt like he was chasing his own tail. He was wading through uncharted waters and soon he would have to decide whether to swim or head back to shore. This was precisely why he had never gotten close to anyone. Too complicated and risky to get involved. Especially since he had more luggage than any terminal at LAX. Yet, by now, he would've run in the other direction if it were anyone other than Ross.

All reason vanished when he was with the handsome detective.

After another hour of going around in circles, James had given up on any hope of finding a solution, or peace of mind. He began the long trek back to the settlement as the sun began setting. The only thing he was positive about was the fact that Avante would eventually come for them if the psycho wasn't found first by the police. Cockroaches always managed to turn up where you didn't want them.

By the time he made it back, most of the houses were dark. James waved at two of the sentries keeping watch until the danger was over. When he climbed the stairs to the porch of Jack's house,

James noticed Ross sitting in one of the rocking chairs holding onto a mug of what smelled like coffee.

"There's a fresh pot inside if you want some," Ross offered.

"No, thanks. I'm good." James took a seat in the rocking chair next to Ross.

The moon was full, blanketing everything in a blue-grey light, making the handsome man even more chiseled. James couldn't win.

"So tell me what got you so worked up that you took a hike into the forest?"

This was why Ross was a detective. Nothing got by him. Keeping things from him was a real pain in the ass, and there was no use in lying. Ross would sniff that out in seconds.

"Trying to decide if I'm doing the right thing," James admitted.

"I'm guessing this has something to do with us."

"Ah, yeah," James grumbled.

"So, what exactly has you worried?"

"The fact that I might be taking advantage of this situation and you." There, the truth. Now deal with it.

Ross set his mug down and looked James straight in the eye. "Do I come across as a man who's easily manipulated?" James knew a rhetorical question when he heard one. "I'm a grown man who has spent the majority of his life on the streets of LA, tracking murderers. If I don't want something to happen, you better believe it won't happen."

"Well, when you put it that way." Interesting to learn he'd been looking at this all wrong.

"Damn straight. I'm no pushover. I have control over my actions. If I didn't want you to touch me, believe me, you would've been out of there the moment you produced the muscle cream. I'm no blushing virgin, and I don't have fantasies what's going on between us is more than temporary. Now get your head on straight because we have bigger issues to deal with then you worrying you're taking advantage of a forty-five-year-old LAPD detective."

Yep, James felt like an idiot. He had been so worried about doing the wrong thing that he hadn't stopped to realize he wasn't the only one involved in this situation and that he had no control over Ross. James had always been, for lack of a better word, the lead in any pseudo-relationship or hook-up.

This situation was foreign to him. Of course he knew plenty of strong, no-nonsense men, but he had never taken one to bed. What did that say about him?

"Point taken," James admitted.

"Good, now that we've relieved your worries," Ross said as he stood. "I think it's time for you to put your money where your mouth is."

James was caught off-guard when Ross reached down, pulled him from his chair, and pushed him up against the wall of the house. Without saying a word, Ross claimed James's mouth in a demanding kiss. He had never been with someone as dominant as he was, and the thought of having a lover who was equally rough-and-tumble made for endless possibilities, and was hot as fuck.

James responded in kind by tearing Ross's button-down wide open, making buttons fly across the deck's boards. He thrust his hands under what was left of the fabric and ran his palms over Ross's muscled chest. James rolled Ross's peaked nipples between his fingers, eliciting a low moan, which only spurred James on.

The moment Ross released James's lips, he latched onto a taut nipple. A firm hand held him in place as he licked and sucked, pulling at the nipple with his teeth. Ross smelled damned good, and James couldn't wait to get his tongue and mouth all over the detective's body.

"Babe, we should take this inside," Ross suggested. "Get out of these clothes."

James was all for that and released his prize. In one quick movement, Ross grabbed his hand and led him through the front door, past the empty living room, and down the hall to their bedroom.

"Now this is much better," Ross growled as he closed and locked the door. "Naked. Now."

James had never been so turned on by being given orders, until now. Actually, he couldn't think of a man who'd had the balls to try to boss him around. He kicked off his boots, shucked his jeans and boxers, and tore his shirt over his head. Ross watched, and with each piece of clothing James removed, the more intensely Ross stared. It was a hell of a boost to James's ego.

Typically, hook-ups were fast, to the point, and frequently over before either had a chance to get their pants off. But this was no hook-up. Not by a long shot.

As Ross's gaze roamed his body, James saw no revulsion when Ross surveyed his scars, only desire. He had been shirtless in front of Ross before, but never naked.

"Your turn, Detective."

Although James had already seen and touched all of Ross's body, with each piece of clothing that hit the floor he gained a completely new appreciation for the male form.

Ross had broad shoulders and a muscled chest and abdomen. That defined V led to a gorgeous cock that James had his mouth only hours ago.

The moment the last piece of fabric fell, James took Ross into his arms and plundered his mouth and lips. His need for the man was riding him hard. Every touch and stroke only made James burn hotter.

"Which way do you want this to play out?" Ross asked as he cupped James's ass cheeks. "Top or bottom?"

James had switched before but tended to be more of a top. Only, in this case, he wanted to feel Ross pressing him into the mattress.

"I'll bottom this time. Then after that, we can take turns."

Oh, yeah. Once would not be anywhere near enough when it came to the smoking hot detective.

"Deal." Ross agreed before pushing James onto the bed. "Condoms and lube?"

"In my bag."

Why did his voice sound so breathless?

Ross picked up James's bag and handed it to him. Once he found the supplies, he threw them onto the bed and tossed his bag back to the floor. There were a lot of things surprising him about Ross lately.

The weight of Ross's body settled over him, as the sensation of warm skin on skin caused him to moan. James needed more. He craved it all. When Ross wrapped his hand around both of their cocks, James had to fight back his orgasm. He was drowning in an all-encompassing kiss while his cock was being stroked between the silky skin of Ross's hard cock and his rough, calloused hand. The contrast served to heighten James's desire.

He broke the kiss and gasped. "Damn, Detective, you have one hell of a touch."

He had seldom been on the receiving end of this type of thorough attention. Most hook-ups didn't bother with foreplay.

"You have no idea." Ross chuckled before diving back in for another kiss.

The stubble on his chin burned James's skin, making him crave more of this sexy man.

Over and over, James was brought to the brink of no return by Ross's hands, tongue, and lips, only to have his lover deny him what James's aching balls needed so badly. His entire body throbbed as he tried to keep his moans low enough not to wake the house.

He reached for the lube and handed it to Ross. With that sexy smile of his, Ross took it and lubed up two fingers.

"How long has it been," Ross asked while circling James's hole.

"More than a few years."

"Okay, I'll take it slow," Ross said before running the tip of his nose up the side of James's neck and sucking his earlobe into Ross's hot, wet mouth.

James's body bowed up off the bed and Ross took that opportunity to slide the end of his finger into him. Ross's talented mouth continued to suck and lick its way across James's neck, coaxing his desire until Ross's finger was buried deep inside of him.

Ross didn't rush. Lazily, he pumped his finger in and out, stretching James while driving him crazy with his tongue on James's nipple. With one small bend of his finger, Ross sent James to the moon. Waves of pleasure poured over him as Ross massaged James without mercy until he had three fingers inside him.

James heard the wrapper being torn and opened his eyes to watch Ross roll the condom down his impressive cock. From the moment this began, Ross never stopped touching him, and James wondered if he was as desperate to keep their connection as James was.

"Ready, babe?" Ross asked.

James could feel the mushroomed head of Ross's cock pressing against his hole.

"Hell, yes."

Ross pushed forward, and inch by inch, slowly he buried himself inside of James. He felt his body stretching around Ross's cock and relished the burn. He waited for his body to adjust to the invasion before he nodded to let Ross know he was ready. Moments later, he was being fucked into the mattress. With every stroke, Ross dragged a moan out of James. Each thrust took his breath away, and even though he was lying down, he felt lightheaded.

Ross set a furious pace, bringing James closer and closer to coming with every thrust. Ross was a thorough lover. His hands and tongue roamed James's body as his cock pounded into him. The sensations collided into a burning need.

"I'm going to come," James gasped out, between moans, and hissed when Ross took hold of his sensitive cock and began pumping in time with the brutal thrusts.

He couldn't stop the freight train running through him as fire raced from his balls and out his cock. Each pulse of his orgasm felt like it was being pulled from his soul, leaving him wrung out and weak. Ross buried himself inside James and came while clenching his teeth as the veins in his neck stood out and his head went back.

James floated on a sea of endorphins barely aware of Ross cleaning them before he was pulled back into those strong arms.

Damn. I could get used to this.

***

Ross woke to James thrashing on the bed. The few words he could make out sounded as if they were being ripped from the man's heart. He was repeating coordinates and asking for an airstrike. Names of men James must've served with echoed through the room as Ross reached for him.

"James… James, wake up. You're having a nightmare." Ross tried to hold James's flailing arms down so neither of them were hurt.

Ross knew that James had been through hell and back while serving overseas. Now, he was seeing some of the fallout. Seeing James in pain wrenched at Ross's gut.

James suddenly stilled, and Ross had a moment to wonder if he was awake or if he had fallen back to sleep before James said, "You can let me go now."

He released the hold he had on him and backed off a few inches to give him room to pull himself together. That wasn't the first time

Ross had woken up to one of James's nightmares, but this had definitely been one of the more violent episodes.

"You okay?" Ross asked as he ran his hand down James's chest.

"Yep."

"Maybe it would help if you talked about it."

He was sure James had heard those words before, but Ross still had to try.

James flew out of the bed so fast that Ross almost lost his balance and fell off the other side.

"I'm fine. I can handle a few bad dreams."

Ross didn't know what was going on, but he was going to damn well find out. This shit was eating away at James, and Ross refused to let it continue.

"Get your ass back in this bed, right now. If you don't want to talk about it, fine, but you will not run away from me. Clear?" He surprised himself with the amount of steel in his voice, but what shocked him even more was the fact that the big guy listened.

James crawled back onto the bed and Ross opened his arms wide so that he could settle next to him. With James's head on his chest, Ross waited for him to make his decision. He was a patient man.

After a few minutes, Ross reached down and pulled the blankets over them before settling in. If James chose not to say a word about the episode, so be it, but it wouldn't stop Ross from trying to find a way to help him.

"What if I told you that I'm responsible for the deaths of five soldiers in my unit?" James asked in a voice that only could be described as self-loathing.

Well, that question had been nowhere on Ross's radar. "I would need more information before I answered."

"We were about half a mile outside a small village in Southern Afghanistan on a routine patrol when we started taking fire. I was hit in the arm but could still fight. After a full hour of engagement, we knew we were outnumbered and we had no backup within a ten mile radius. I gave the order for everyone to bug out. Three members of the team made it back to the Stryker, while two others and I were providing cover fire. Once they were safe, the rest of us began working our way to them. The turret was manned and returning fire, so we made a break for the vehicle. We were less than twenty feet away when a mortar round hit the Stryker. The next thing I knew, I was waking up in a hospital in Germany and was told it was over a week after we'd been ambushed. That's when I learned that I was the only one found alive."

The thought of James so close to dying made Ross's mouth go dry, but he was having a hard time assigning blame to James.

"I'm so sorry that happened to your unit."

"But?" James asked without looking up.

"I'm honestly sorry that happened to you and the men you served with."

"You're not going to try to convince me it wasn't my fault, like the doctors, the shrinks, my commanding officer, and Jack?"

"No. If you believe you're guilty, there's nothing I can possibly say to change your mind. But I do have a question."

"Okay." James's voice held uncertainty.

"What would have happened if you hadn't given the order to draw back?"

When James didn't answer, Ross continued. "You were taking fire and outnumbered. Whether they were in the Stryker or not, it would've been hit and blown up. So, say they weren't in the Stryker. What would've happened after it blew up?"

"We would've continued fighting until help arrived."

"But you said there wasn't any backup within ten miles of your team. Would you have been able to hold out that long?"

"We would've put up one hell of a fight."

"I have no doubt that you would have. Now, answer me honestly. Would your team have been able to hold them off until help arrived?"

Ross could feel James's body tense.

"I told them to go back to the Stryker."

"You did because you were trying to save them in an impossible situation." Ross left it at that, figuring he had stirred up enough pain for one evening. "Why don't you try to get some rest? If you want, we can talk more in the morning."

Ross pulled James closer and settled back against the headboard. It took a while, but when the full weight of James's body finally relaxed into Ross, he slid down and curled his arms around James before closing his eyes.

Ross wondered how long this amazing man had been blaming himself for his unit's death when he'd done everything possible to keep them alive, and in the end, he was lucky to be alive.

Survivor's guilt sucked.

CHAPTER 11

James looked up from the forms he had built and set into place for the footings for a new prefabricated house Jack had ordered. Ross was walking toward him with two bottles of water. It was the morning after they'd had sex and James was conflicted over Ross's reaction to his admission of guilt.

"Hey, how goes the footings?" Ross asked as he neared. His piercing blue eyes seemed brighter in the sunlight.

"Setting up good," James replied. "What're you up to?"

"Heading out to check on one of Jack's sensors. It stopped working a few days ago." Wanna come along?"

Since he'd done all he could on the footings, and alone time with Ross sounded perfect, he said, "Sure." He caught one of the water bottles Ross threw. "Let's go."

He climbed up out of the hole and followed Ross over to one of the sheds, the entire time admiring a perfect jean-covered ass. The detective was like a magnet, drawing him in with an invisible tether.

"If you stare any harder you're going to burn a hole in my pants," Ross joked as he stopped beside one of the side-by-side ATVs. "Hop on."

James raised his brow and smiled. "That's an open invitation?"

Ross laughed. James liked the sound of it.

"The ATV, smartass."

"Just checking, since I'm open to offers."

James couldn't help himself. This give-and-take with Ross made him happier than he had been in a long time. It felt freeing.

"Get in," Ross said as he slapped James on the ass.

"Not helping," James growled while climbing in.

Ross laughed even harder.

He grabbed the backpack off the roof and got in behind the wheel, pushed a button on the GPS and it blinked to life. Entering the coordinates took only a moment and then they were off.

As soon as they hit the forest, Ross reached over and took hold of James's hand. They twined their fingers together without saying a word. He never held hands, unless it was with an injured combat brother. It felt oddly satisfying. Hell, he was cuddling and holding hands. What was next, getting matching shirts that said, "I'm his" with a damn arrow on it?

Ross was making James second-guess everything he knew and had done. He wasn't sure he was ready for that. Especially since he was leaving LA the moment this shit was done and Avante was either behind bars or dead.

James wasn't looking for anything long-term. But still, he sat there holding hands like a goofy teenager.

For the next hour, before the terrain became too treacherous to continue with the ATV, they'd bumped along the trail over rocks and branches, following the directions the GPS spit out every five minutes.

"We'll have to hike from here," James said. "It doesn't look to be too far over the next ridge."

Ross grabbed the backpack, slung it over his shoulders, and began leading the way. The air felt fresher up there and the colors brighter. James even noticed birds flying from tree to tree. Had he ever stopped to notice something as simple as a bird?

"Beautiful, isn't it?" Ross put to words what James had been thinking.

"Yep," James agreed. "I don't think I've ever slowed down long enough to appreciate it."

"I know what you mean." Ross nodded, and James could understand how easy it was for him being consumed in his work to miss the finer things. Ross needed more of a life outside of the grind of being a detective in a huge city.

They continued trekking upward, never going more than a few minutes without brushing each other's hand or arm. They seemed to crave the contact. It felt so natural and so foreign at the same time. He'd never wanted to touch someone this much. Hell, he had never wanted to be touched this much.

James felt as though he'd been thrown onto a whole new playing field. The rules had changed and the players chosen, but he wasn't certain he wanted to join this team. The dilemma burned through his brain. He glanced down at their clasped hands and thought he'd live in the moment. Right now he didn't need to make a decision. He needed to take what was on offer and enjoy it for the little time they had together.

"There it is," Ross said as he pointed straight ahead.

Attached to what had to be a six-foot tall green pole was a box with a small antenna sticking out the top. Ross removed the backpack and dug out a small tool kit and a new battery pack to hook up to the small solar panel mounted above the box.

"You sure you know what you are doing?" James asked.

"Jack gave me a rundown before we left. If it's more complicated than we can handle, he'll have to come up here himself."

"Deal. I'll get the cover off for you," James said before reaching for a screwdriver. "Shouldn't take too long."

Together they worked in unison, repairing the sensor. James saw that Ross knew things James didn't and vice versa. James had missed the unity he'd had with his combat brothers and when they'd worked together like a well-oiled machine.

With a little bit of finagling, they were able to hook up the new battery pack to the solar panels. Once they had everything back in place, Ross stood, preparing to head back down the mountain. But James wasn't ready to return to reality quite yet.

"Why don't we take a break up here? It's a hell of a view," he suggested while waving his hand out in front of him at the small valley below.

Ross looked around and pointed at a rock outcropping and said, "Sounds good. I brought lunch."

"You're telling me this now? I'm starving," James grumbled.

"Poor baby, you're withering away to nothing in your two hundred sixty-pound frame."

"Two-fifty." James laughed, remembering the other day when Officer Webb had called in Ross after James had "disagreed" with a pimp who was hitting one of his working girls. "Shut up and sit your ass down."

Ross smirked but sat and began rooting through the backpack. James sat down behind the detective and pulled him into the V of his legs before leaning back against a tree trunk. Ross said nothing, but he smiled and handed James a cellophane-wrapped ham and cheese sandwich and another bottle of water.

For the next thirty minutes, they ate in companionable silence, with the view of the valley below, and the rolling hills in the distance serving as entertainment. Cardinals sang and played in the trees around them, making the place feel damn near fictional. James half expected some prince to ride by any second.

"What's got you laughing?" Ross asked.

James hadn't realized he'd been laughing. He'd been so relaxed he let his inner musings leak out, something he rarely did.

He decided to answer with the truth even if it made him look crazy. "It seems too perfect here. Like the ending of a chick flick or fairytale."

"I was thinking a few people with pickaxes and singing a catchy tune should be wandering by any minute," Ross admitted before laughing and leaning further back into James's arms. "It's nice to know this exists in reality. Even if we only have a few hours to enjoy it."

They relaxed back into a comfortable silence. James had his arms wrapped around Ross's chest, and leaned his head back against the tree trunk. It seemed like such a simple thing, but this moment meant more than the sum of its parts.

He almost felt normal, if he even knew what normal was. From the beginning of his life, or more importantly, from the onset of his understanding of his surroundings, the world had been skewed by his parents' beliefs and the Founder's vision. When James managed to break free of them, he walked into a different kind of hell. One where life was expendable, and every time new orders came in, soldiers died. Airplanes that brought in fresh soldiers also flew out the caskets. He couldn't help but feel that the loss of life didn't matter since they could always bring more to replace the fallen.

Cities and towns destroyed, families separated or killed. The sounds of bombs and gunfire going off was a constant gruesome lullaby. Over the years, he had lost count of how many teammates had come and gone. It somehow felt easier not connecting on a more human level, knowing each day could be your last.

From IEDs to ambush, and suicide bomber to child soldiers, James had seen and managed to live through it all. He could not say the same for everyone.

Ross leaned his head back onto James's shoulder, and he couldn't help but kiss the handsome detective's temple. The two of them out here on their own with only birds for company lent itself to a kind of intimacy James had never known.

He no longer looked forward to the day they would have to say goodbye to this. The day he would have to leave Ross and everyone behind. The optimism he'd had over his decision to leave was waning, and he was beginning to wonder if it had been the best plan for his happiness.

***

After they returned to the compound, Ross watched as James returned to working on the footings. He had been quiet since they'd stopped for lunch, and Ross wondered what had changed. Everything had been light and casual up to that point, and he thought they had been enjoying each other's company. It appeared he'd been wrong.

"So how did it go?" Jack asked as neared the new construction site. "I haven't had a chance to go in and check the system yet."

"It was charging when we left," Ross replied, "so I imagine that's a good sign."

"Great, great. I'll check on it later," Jack said. "You got a minute?"

"I've got a whole ton of minutes at the moment waiting for news. What's up?"

"Let's go have a drink on the porch and get out of this sun." Instead of waiting for Ross to answer, Jack walked away.

Ross swore he was not going to be roped into building cinderblock walls again.

He followed, his mind running the gambit from Jack asking him and his family to leave because it was becoming too dangerous, to Jack dating his sister. Ross wasn't blind. He saw the looks the two had been giving each other since day one.

After they sat down on the porch chairs, Jack reached into a cooler set between the rockers and pulled out two cold beers. He removed the caps and handed one to Ross.

"So, what are your plans?" Jack asked.

Ross took a long swig of his beer before answering. "I intend to make Avante pay for everything he's done, and take care of my family." He thought that would be obvious.

"No, no, I mean, what are your plans for James?" Jack asked as if talking about their relationship was any of his business.

"Look, we've already had this talk. I appreciate that you're his friend, but—"

"He's changed. James isn't the same person I scraped off the sand in Afghanistan, or the one I've known for the many years after that."

"You were the one that found him?" Ross asked. Things were getting clearer about the ties between Jack and James.

"Yeah. I'm happy to hear he told you about what happened over there. He doesn't share that part of his life easily," Jack stated and took another drink. "Still carries around the guilt."

"There's nothing he could've done, Ross said.

"I know that, and so do you, but James's view on the subject is another matter. Because of it, he's determined to avoid any happiness that might come his way."

Strangely, that kind of made sense. He probably figured if the men of his unit couldn't experience any happiness ever again, then neither would he.

"You said that he's changed. How?" Ross asked.

"He didn't hightail it out of here after you two had sex," Jack stated bluntly.

"How do you know about that?" If he had the rooms in his house under surveillance, Ross was going to beat him into the ground. Hell, his sister and niece were here too.

"My bedroom is next door, remember, and that bed squeaks."

Shit. The thought of Jack listening to them was all kinds of wrong, but it was infinitely better than surveillance or his sister hearing.

"He's stuck here with the rest of us until Avante is found. But, he's made it clear he intends to leave LA as soon as this is done."

"Oh, trust me, if James wanted to leave no one on this earth would be able to stop him. Short of tying him up." Jack had a strange smile on his face when he said the last part.

"Tell me you haven't tied him up before."

"I could tell you that, but it would be a lie," Jack said. "We're getting off topic here. This isn't about me."

"Whatever," Ross huffed.

"We're talking about James and you."

"Fine. How else has he changed?"

"Hell, he's smiling, and not in that I'm-about-to-rip-off-your-head way. I've never seen him happy. Don't get me wrong, he's always been a good guy. But stoic, you know."

"Yeah, that sounds about right. When I first met him, he acted the same way. He tends to be self-destructive."

"Oh, yeah. Been that way since the day I met him. Nevertheless, he's allowed himself to be happy with you. It must be one hell of a battle going on inside him right now. A part telling him he doesn't deserve it, and the other craving it most of all."

Ross had to admit, he had never thought of it that way. The internal struggle James had to be going through was heartbreaking.

"Maybe it would be best if I backed off. I don't want to cause him any extra issues." Even saying the words felt wrong.

"Is that what you want to do?"

"No, but I will if I have to." Ross would never be the man to cause James more pain.

"Don't. Trust me when I say, this is good for him. James has never had someone strong enough to challenge the status quo. And from what I've been told, neither have you."

"How did this turn out to be about me? I thought we were talking about James."

"Tomato, tomaato," Jack said while waving his beer bottle around. "Point is, you've been stuck in your own ways as well."

Ross didn't even bother to dispute it. For years, his sister had told him the same thing. "I've had responsibilities."

"Yeah. I'm told you're exceptionally responsible."

Ross didn't know if that was a shot or not. "Someone has to be."

"Hey, I'm not knocking ya. I'm responsible for all these people. I understand the feeling of wanting to be free to make choices without using logic and preparing for all possible scenarios." Before Ross could respond, Jack said, "Back on track, we're here to talk about James."

"Have you been diagnosed with ADD?" Ross had to ask, what with the way the guy was bouncing around subjects.

"Funny. Funny," Jack replied. "James will have a hard time talking you in circles. Now, what's the game plan?"

"Game plan?" Ross took the last swig of beer from his bottle and took another out of the cooler. He needed alcohol for this conversation.

"Yeah, so what are you going to do to keep James around after this blows over?" Jack asked as if Ross somehow had the magic answer.

What was he going to do? Did he want to do anything? This was supposed to be temporary. He had no long-term plan. Hell, Ross didn't have any plans past catching Avante.

"Well, I can see you need some time to think about it," Jack said before emptying his beer. "I'll leave you to work it out. I'm sure you'll come up with something."

Jack stood and started back down the porch stairs without saying another word, leaving Ross to think about shit he didn't want to tackle.

CHAPTER 12

"How is it possible for Avante to still be on the streets?" Ross asked no one in particular.

His frustration at the situation was riding close to the surface. His sister and niece shouldn't have to hide out indefinitely.

James, Wallflower, Ross, Jack, and Jac sat around the kitchen table while Wallflower's seventeen-year-old sister, Rainbow, was out playing with Becca at the small playground on the other side of the settlement.

Ross was stunned as he read through the reports laid out in front of him. It had been almost a week since they'd gone into hiding and it seemed the LAPD were no further along in apprehending Avante. It seemed as if someone was dragging their feet, and given what had happened with Sparks, corruption up the chain was possible. But Avante had been "disowned" by his mob boss, stripped of his money and power. What benefit would anyone yield in keeping him alive and on the streets?

Ross'd been in contact with Bev who told him they were close to figuring out how far the corruption had spread, but not having Avante in custody, or even a clue where he was, appeared to imply something completely different.

Wallflower, hacker extraordinaire, had given him more information than Bev had, or shared, which led to the sick feeling building in his stomach.

"Do you honestly think she had anything to do with this?" Jac asked Ross. She had to know how devastating that would be for him.

"I don't know. It's possible," Ross was loath to admit. "But I haven't spoken with her in a few days. Maybe things have changed."

Since Avante was still at large, nothing much *had* changed.

"We should prepare for worst-case scenario just in case," James suggested. "I don't want to be an asshole, but I would feel a hell of a lot better if we consider Bev an unknown at this point."

Had his oldest friend betrayed him? Had Bev been working with Sparks to help Avante get away? Were they hunting them even now? Questions piled up with no answers in sight. This day couldn't get much worse.

Wallflower's phone rang.

She looked down at it and said, "Wonder what Rainbow wants?" She pressed the answer button. "What's up, sis?" she asked. Ross noticed her demeanor change almost immediately and her face drained of blood.

He went on alert at the same time as James.

"He wants me to put the call on speaker," she said.

Shit. Ross nodded and Wallflower tapped the button with a trembling finger as tears began running down her cheeks.

"Hello, Ross. Bet you thought you'd seen the last of me?" Avante's voice rang out with an air of self-satisfaction.

Ross wanted to be the one to jam his fist right down Avante's throat.

Jac gasped and began to cry knowing Becca was with Rainbow.

"What have you done with Rainbow and Becca?" Ross demanded. He needed more information and to keep Avante talking.

James and Jack were making hand signals to each other as if they were having a conversation. Ross could hear the wind and birds in the background of Avante's call, but nothing solid or specific to give him a sense of where they were.

"Straight to the point. You were never one for subtlety, Detective. Becca is safe, and will remain happy and healthy for now. As for Rainbow, she appears to be doing much better now that we're here, considering she's the one who led us to you."

"Rainbow?" Wallflower asked in disbelief. Her voice shook as she stared down at her phone. "You're lying."

Abruptly the voice on the phone changed to that of her sister. "Honestly, Wallflower. Aren't you the smart one, the hacker with all the moves? Bet you didn't see this one coming."

"But why?" Wallflower asked.

"Do you think I want to hang out in the middle of nowhere digging holes and planting gardens? That's what the supermarket is for. You and Dad brought me out here without ever asking me if I wanted to become some messed-up survivalist. I want to be in the city, go to parties, and dance in clubs and wear stilettos, not rubber boots. Thanks to you leaving Avante's information lying around, I found the perfect way out and the money to fund my own life wherever I want to live."

Ross had met Rainbow only a couple of times, and never would've suspected the teenager was capable of this. By the look on Wallflower's face, neither had she.

"You see, Detective," Avante said, "I couldn't get to you because of all those yahoos with guns around. So imagine my surprise when one of them offered to bring the kid to me."

"What do you want?" Ross asked, barely holding onto his anger and terror.

He needed to face this logically if he was to get Becca back.

"To start, you begging for your life," Avante growled like a caged animal. "You've cost me too much. Now I'm going to take it out of your flesh, pound by pound. There will be a vehicle waiting for you on the main road at highway marker sixty-eight. Don't be late. And Detective, do come alone. I wouldn't want anything to happen to that beautiful niece of yours."

The line went dead and the room fell silent.

Ross looked at his sister who was softly crying in Jack's arms. "I'll get her back, Jac. I swear it."

They needed a plan. Avante would have his crew with him, so Ross would need more people. But it was one thing to ask these people to hide them here, and another to ask them to risk their lives.

As if reading his mind, Jack said, "I'll start asking for volunteers to go with us to get Becca back. That won't be a problem."

"Their lives would be in danger. I can't ask that of them."

"Who says you were asking? Some of these folks are itching to get a chance at Avante. Everyone's fallen in love with that little girl and will want her back," Jack explained while still holding onto Ross's sister.

"Okay, but they have to be doing this for their own reasons."

"Done," Jack agreed as he led Jac over to a large cushioned chair in the living room. "Wallflower, get Jac a bottle of water, please."

Ross looked over at James who was already staring at him.

"I have to go, unarmed. It's the only way to keep Becca safe until you guys get her out."

"I will find you," James stated through gritted teeth.

"I never had a doubt."

***

James watched as Ross rode off on one of Jack's ATV's to meet up with Avante. No matter how many times he'd been reassured, James couldn't help but find flaws in the hastily developed plan. Avante had the advantage at this point, and there were too many opportunities for Ross and Becca to be killed.

Once Wallflower snapped out of her shock, she outfitted Ross with GPS trackers hidden in the soles of his boots. The small red dot on the screen confirmed it was working, but did nothing to calm James. Sure, they could track Ross, but James feared it would be too late by the time they got to him. Ross had said he was willing to take the risk if there was any chance of getting Becca back, and James understood that. He didn't like it, but he would've done the same thing.

While the spotters kept watch and the sensors tracked Ross, James, Jack, and a half-dozen men and women from the community, climbed onto their ATV's. With Jack's knowledge of the area, they hoped to be able to follow Avante and his men back to where ever they were hiding without being seen. James figured Avante couldn't go near any populated areas knowing there was a manhunt on his trail. He and his minions had to be hiding somewhere up in the mountains.

It infuriated him that Rainbow was able to take Becca on a supposed ATV ride without supervision. Nevertheless, what was done was done. Avante had made his move. Now it was James's turn.

From a tablet, they watched the visual sensors set all over the area as Ross neared the highway marker where a black SUV sat waiting for him. Ross stopped a few feet away from the vehicle and got off his ATV. The front passenger door opened and a large bald man got out with a handgun trained on Ross. James's stomach clenched.

After the guy took a long look around him, he opened the back passenger door. Avante stepped out and took the gun before approaching Ross. James could see that a few words were exchanged, and by all indications, Avante was not happy with what was being said. James couldn't help but grin, knowing Ross would be defiant even in the face of that psycho's wrath.

Without warning, Avante raised the gun and pistol-whipped Ross. Ross collapsed and lay unmoving on the ground. Everything inside of James demanded he take the bastard out. If he had a sniper's rifle, he might've considered it, but they needed to get Becca back first.

"We will get them back," Jack said, and up until that moment, James hadn't realized he'd been growling.

"That bastard is mine."

First, he would assure Becca and Ross were safe, and then he would rain death down on the man who had terrorized his family. There was no time to analyze that shit right now, but he was damn certain of how he felt.

Ross had given James a part of his life back. They may not have had the chance to finish their discussion, and perhaps James had been avoiding it, but he had to admit Ross had made him look at his past differently. That didn't mean James felt he was innocent of blame, but it helped him to see the events more clearly.

"They're on the move," Wallflower announced, sparking everyone into action.

Each person was armed and carried first aid kits. Half of the people living in the community were retired military, which made James more hopeful that all this would end without any innocents being hurt.

Using the GPS, they followed Avante at a distance, making sure to never be within sight of the vehicle. The entire time James seethed as the vision of Ross being thrown into the back of the SUV like a bag of garbage replayed in his mind. There would be no place Avante could hide. James would never stop. Jac and Becca deserved to live in peace, and he would make sure that happened.

After thirty minutes, the signal stopped moving. They abandoned their ATVs and closed in on foot. The sun hung low in the sky by the time they reached the location where Avante had made camp.

There were three tents tall enough for a person to stand up in. A few of Avante's men milled around the two vehicles while others stood guarding two of the tents, making it easier to determine that Becca and Ross were in either one of them.

The plan was to get Becca out of there long before things heated up, but they weren't sure which of the tents she was being held in.

A soft hiss had James turning his attention back to Wallflower who was staring at the vehicles. Movement caught his eyes as Rainbow came walking out from behind the third tent.

They were still too far away to hear what was being said, but by the way her arms were slicing through the air it was easy to tell she was pissed. One of Avante's men yelled something and pointed to the furthest tent with Becca's backpack in his hand. The teenager stomped her foot, ripped the bag out of the guy's hand, and stormed her way over to the tent before flipping him off and going inside.

"Now we know which tent Becca's in," Jack confirmed what James had already been thinking.

"Rainbow is mine," Wallflower said softly. "It's one thing to not want this kind of life. It's completely another to sacrifice a child as a means to go about getting it."

"We get Becca first," James said. "Whatever goes on between you and your sister is your business. But if Rainbow comes between Becca and me, I *will* remove the threat."

He didn't like the idea of shooting Rainbow, but knowing the teenager had sacrificed Becca for her own benefit assuaged some of his guilt.

"Understood," Wallflower agreed.

"Good. Let's go."

The team broke up into two groups. One led by Jack, the other by James. Jack's group would stay out of sight while surrounding the area and waiting for the signal to attack. James and Wallflower would go for Becca while the rest of their group covered them.

As soon as the sun had set, they made their move. They neared the back of the tent they hoped held Becca, their black clothing helping them blend into the darkness.

"I want my mommy," Becca's angry voice surprised James. He would have figured she would have been too scared to demand anything. Then again, she was her mother's daughter, and Jac could kick ass.

"Your mommy isn't here and if you ever want to see her again you better be good," Rainbow threatened in a sickly sweet voice. "I don't have to put up with your shit."

"You said a bad word," Becca was quick to point out.

"Like I fucking care, brat."

James could see Wallflower's hands clenching into fists as she listened to her sister threaten and swear at a small child. He reached out, placed his hand over top of hers and shook his head. Wallflower had to push her emotions aside until they got Becca out. She nodded her understanding and flexed her fingers to loosen them.

"I'm thirsty," Becca was not giving Rainbow any breaks. James loved that kid.

"So," Rainbow spat out. "What do you want me to do about it?"

"You have to get me something to drink," Becca explained as if she were talking to a younger child then herself.

James couldn't help but wonder if she got her calm demeanor from her uncle.

"Too bad, kid. I'm not in the mood to take orders from you." Rainbow laughed as if the thought of getting the kid a bottle of water was hilarious.

"I'm thirsty...I'm thirsty...I'm thirsty," Becca chanted.

"Stop it," Rainbow growled.

"I'm thirsty...thirsty...thirsty."

Go, girl. It couldn't be said enough how much he loved this kid.

"Fine. I'll go get you some water, just shut up," Rainbow hissed.

A chair creaked and her footsteps headed away from the tent. Once he heard the tent flap close, he pulled out his tactical knife and sliced into the back of the tent like a hot knife through butter. He hoped that he didn't scare Becca into making a noise to alert the guard.

Thankfully, she didn't make a peep as James crawled through the cut fabric. She was sitting on a small blow-up mattress in the far corner clutching Puppy in her arms. James raised his finger to his lips and Becca smiled wide before running over and jumping into his arms.

Without saying a word, silently, he backed out of the tent. Wallflower crawled inside to wait for her sister. All they needed was for her to sound the alarm before they made their move.

James held Becca close to his chest and disappeared into the darkness. When he reached the rest of the team, he finally loosened his hold to look down at the little girl.

"I knew you and Uncle Ross would find me. Rainbow isn't nice." Becca frowned.

"No, she isn't," James agreed. "These people are going to take you back to Mommy, okay?"

"Okay. I miss Mommy,." Becca said as she squeezed Puppy tighter.

"Mommy misses you, too." James hugged her close before handing her over to Peggy, the wife of a fellow Army soldier.

Becca was safe. Now it was time for him to get his man back.

Wallflower returned moments later with a bound and gagged Rainbow in tow. The fat lip she was sporting evidence that Rainbow had not come easily.

"Okay, let's—"

James began but was cut off by a vehicle coming over the hill and nearing Avante's campsite.

Everyone hunkered down and watched as the last person James had ever expected, stepped out of the car.

"This complicates things."

CHAPTER 13

Ross shook his head trying to clear the fog from his brain, only to come away in more pain than he'd started. Avante hadn't held back when he'd hit him with the butt end of a gun. Ross had regained consciousness only a short while ago, and suspected he'd been kicked in the ribs a few times while he'd been out. He was having a hard time taking a deep breath and straightening his back.

His hands were tied behind his back and he was secured around an old fence post. Ross had not seen Becca and hoped James and the team had already gotten her away from here. Ross had been working on the ropes since he woke up and was finally starting to make some headway with the razor blade he had hidden in the band of his watch.

The risks of this plan were becoming all too real. As he had predicted, Avante would try to cause Ross as much pain as possible while Ross held out until Becca was free. If he had to use his dying moments to ensure Avante did not walk away from here, Ross would gladly do it. His family deserved none of this.

If there was one thing Ross knew for a fact, if he should happen to fail in stopping Avante, James would not. He had sworn it to Ross before he had left to meet up with the psycho. Even though he hadn't wanted to discuss the possibility of being killed, the reality of it was staring him in the face.

Ross heard the rumble and saw the headlights of another vehicle pulling up outside the tent where he was being held. A single door opened and shut before footsteps started heading his way.

"What the fuck're you doing here?" Avante snarled.

"Someone has to make sure this is done right this time around. No more screw-ups."

Ross recognized that voice, but was having a hard time wrapping his head around the implications. Two sets of footsteps headed his way, and it wasn't until the tent flaps were pulled aside that he had his confirmation.

"Hello, Ross."

"Mr. Mayor."

"John, please." The bastard had the guts to smile down on him as if they were passing in the rotunda of City Hall. "Why couldn't you have left this alone?" The mayor asked. "Your brother-in-law was a scumbag who got what he deserved."

"When Avante brought my sister and niece into this, the game changed. They're my first priority," Ross growled.

The mayor turned to look at Avante with disgust. "I told you to leave that bitch and her kid alone. Taking her was going to cause problems. Now we're here, and on a damn election year."

"Sorry to screw up your re-election plans." Ross laughed at the audacity of the dirty mayor worrying about an election when he was more than likely here to kill him.

The first strike from Avante he had expected. The second and third, not so much. The metallic taste in his mouth confirmed his lip had split and a few molars were loose. Ross spit blood out, aiming it onto the mayor's designer shoe. The man jumped back as if he'd been stuck with a cattle prod.

"Shit, these cost more than you're worth, asshole," he hissed, as he pulled out a white handkerchief and began rubbing the blood away.

The whole thing was so absurd that Ross wondered if he was hallucinating. Maybe he'd been hit on the head harder than he thought.

"So, you're dirty as hell, John. How long have you been sucking up to the mob?" Ross asked with distain. "You know, when they get tired of paying you, or you aren't of any use to them anymore, you'll be the next one they find in the gutter."

"Oh, I'll get what's coming to me. The Governor's Mansion sounds about right, and who knows how far I can go from there. Senator. President, even."

When Ross laughed, the mayor took a shot at him.

Ross spit out another mouthful of blood and said, "You're disgusting. Does Bev know she's sleeping with the enemy? And do you know you bet on the wrong horse with Avante?"

The look of confusion on the mayor's face was comical.

"He didn't tell you? He's been cut off from his mob boss. Banished, cast out, broke, and on the shortlist for disposal." Ross knew he was pushing it, but he needed the two assholes to shift their attention away from him. "Wonder how you're going to line your pockets now."

He got exactly for what he had been hoping. John turned on Avante. "What the hell is he talking about? Are you broke?"

Avante didn't look so sure of himself, and seeing the change come over his ugly mug was satisfying. "It's only a temporary situation."

"Things get permanent fast when it comes to the mob." Ross couldn't help but stoke the flames.

"Shut the fuck up," Avante bellowed as spit flew from his mouth.

"What about our deal?" John asked. "You said you could get me a meeting with Bishop."

Bishop? That was a new player Ross hoped he lived long enough to pass along. Likely, it stood for the B. Gen who had cleared out Avante's account.

"Isn't he the one that cleaned out your accounts and took every possession?" Ross asked to ascertain it was indeed the same guy.

Avante pointed his gun at him. "If you don't shut up, I will put a bullet in your skull."

"Fuck him, be more worried about me, asshole." The mayor wasn't playing anymore.

"You won't need a meeting with Bishop when I'm running the show," Avante blustered. "I have plans for LA, and if you ever talk to me in that tone again I will end you."

It seemed that the mayor wasn't the only one with delusions of grandeur.

"A takeover?" Ross laughed. "You, the boss? Holy shit, have you been snorting your own supply?"

Avante raised his fist to deliver another blow when the sound of a gunshot broke the silence outside of the tent. The panic in John's eyes would've been fulfilling if it weren't for the gun he had pulled out from under his suit jacket.

"What the hell is that?" John asked.

"James." Ross smiled wide even with his busted lip.

Now that the two rocket scientists were occupied, Ross returned to cutting through the ropes around his wrists. He had already nicked himself countless times but refused to stop, even if there was blood dripping down on his hands.

More gunfire erupted around them. Avante stormed over to Ross and jammed the barrel of his gun against the side of his head.

"No one is saving your ass. Not if you're a corpse when they get here."

A shot rang out and it took a second for Ross to realize Avante was falling to the ground. He looked up to find James standing in the open flap of the tent, but his relief didn't last long.

"Drop your gun or I will shoot him." John stood only a foot away, with his gun pointed at Ross's head.

He was getting fuckin' tired of people trying to kill him.

"Shoot him," Ross ordered. This had to end here and now. "Shoot him."

Instead, James lowered his gun and threw it onto the ground.

Shit.

James looked at Ross and something flipped inside of him. Love.

John turned his gun on James. "You should've shot me when you had the chance. Thought you Army guys were smarter than that."

Everything from that moment on seemed to happen in slow motion. As John aimed his gun at James, the ropes tying Ross to the pole finally gave way. Clutching the razor blade in his hand, Ross dove in front of John's gun while using the blade to cut across the mayor's throat. The gun went off and a searing pain shot through Ross's abdomen. He and John hit the ground at the same time.

The next thing Ross knew, he was being held in James's arms, and he was pressing down on Ross's stomach with his shirt.

"Die," a voice gurgled and Ross turned his head in time to see John clutching at his bleeding throat, picking up the gun. He took aim once again as James covered Ross's body with his own in an attempt to protect him.

Another shot exploded, but Ross didn't feel an impact to James's body. "Are you hit?"

"No." James raised his head slightly to look around, before uncovering Ross's body.

Ross looked over to find the mayor on the ground, a bullet hole through the center of his chest. Ross turned his head in the opposite direction to find Bev standing in open flap of the tent, a gun in her hand.

"Bev. You're here."

"Yeah, I didn't get a chance to tell you," James said. "Bev, we need first aid and a chopper to airlift Ross to the nearest trauma center. He has a gunshot to his abdomen and multiple head traumas."

"Becca?" Ross had to make sure she was safe. "You got her out?"

"Long gone before the first shot was fired," James assured.

Ross was so relieved that he didn't notice how weak he was becoming until he found himself fighting to keep his eyes open.

"Hey, stay awake for me," James demanded. "You're not going anywhere now that you made me fall in love with you."

Ross tried to speak, to tell James that he loved him too, but he couldn't form the words. The next moment James was shaking and yelling at him to stay awake, but no matter how hard he tried, he was losing the battle.

With his last bit of strength, Ross cupped the side of James's face before everything went dark.

CHAPTER 14

James sat staring at the plain beige wall for so long that he started thinking the worse. Bells and phones were going off constantly up and down the halls as nurses and doctors discussed various patients. Finn and Miguel had brought him a change of clothes, and when he changed in a hospital bathroom, he nearly cried at the amount of Ross's blood that covered his discarded clothing.

The rest of the Gates crew plus Jac, Becca, Jack, Bev, and a contingent of LAPD officers and detectives, had been in and out all night as they waited for word on Ross's condition. Many of them brought food, but that sat untouched on the side table in the waiting room.

As it turned out, Bev had grown suspicious of the mayor and had been on a team that tailed him out to the mountains. Sparks's body had washed up hundreds of miles to the north on Pismo Beach a couple days after they'd ran from the safe house. Apparently, the mayor had started acting irrationally, disappearing at all hours, never explaining where he had been. When Bev sounded the alarm to her higher-ups, she outed their relationship in the process.

James knew the guilt of being responsible for someone's death, but he still couldn't imagine having to kill your lover to save your partner.

Time passed, and they waited. And they waited some more. A nurse from the surgery team had come out and told them Ross had extensive internal injuries and had lost a lot of blood. That had been hours ago. James looked down at his hands and though he had already scrubbed them twice, all he could see was them covered in Ross's blood. His mind couldn't erase the sight of Ross jumping in front of the bullet meant for James.

Ross had trusted James to get him out of there safe, and he had failed.

"Don't get that look in your eyes," Jack said as he came to stand beside James.

"What the hell are you talking about?" He was not in the mood to play twenty questions.

"Guilt. It's written all over your face. This is not your fault. None of this," Jack assured.

"If I hadn't dropped my gun and shot the asshole, this wouldn't't've happened."

"From what I hear you didn't have a choice. He was pointing a gun at Ross's head."

"I should have been able to do something," James responded while crossing his arms over his chest.

"Don't give me that closed arms wall shit. You can't control everything. Bad things happen to good people no matter how hard you try to stop it."

James knew Jack wasn't only talking about today's events. "You know, when I told Ross how my team had died, he didn't even condemn me."

"See, how many times–"

"But he didn't clear me of any guilt either. Ross had asked me questions and showed me that perhaps it was not as clear-cut as I'd believed. Everyone before had either fallen into one of two camps: those that blamed me, and those who were quick to say I'm innocent. No one ever bothered to ask me questions and talked me through it."

"He's a good man," Jack said with a look of respect in his eyes.

"Yeah, he is."

Before either could continue their conversation, a doctor wearing blue scrubs walked into the waiting room. "Family of Detective Ross."

Practically the entire room stood. "How is he?" Jac asked as Becca slept in Marian's arms. "Is he alive?"

"He's made it through surgery. The next few days are crucial, but we believe he's out of danger." James respected the compassion the doc was showing Jac.

"Thank you for everything you've done for my brother." Jac began crying in what had to be relief. Hell, James was ready to do the same thing. "When can we see him?"

"He's out of recovery and is in the Intensive Care Unit. Sorry folks, but only two visitors are allowed in at a time. I'll be happy to lead you back."

Jac wrapped her arm around James and said, "We're ready."

James hadn't said a word. He was replaying the words "out of danger" in his head. The two of them followed the doctor through the swinging doors, down a long hallway, and up to a glassed room. There were several glassed rooms in the unit. A nurse sat directly outside the window to Ross's room in front of a monitor.

"He'll be out of it for a while, but you're welcome to sit in his room and wait," the doctor told them as he reviewed his tablet, which James assumed held Ross's chart.

James finally found his voice, which sounded scratchy when he spoke. "Thank you again." However, he refused to take his eyes off the still figure in the bed.

"You're welcome. He's a fighter," the doctor stated before walking away

James could not help but smile at that. If only the doctor knew the half of it. Ross was an exceptional person and would never give up.

Jac was trembling. "He's going to be okay, honey," James tried to assure her. Unabashedly, he had insinuated himself into the family. On the other hand, Jac had come right to him to go to the ICU.

"But look at all the tubes and machines. Something can still happen to him." Tears rolled down Jac's face.

"We have to be strong for him. Ross needs us to do the heavy lifting now."

Jac straightened her back and wiped her eyes. "You're right, we need to take care of him this time. He's always been the strong one, now we have to be stronger." She released James and walked over to Ross's bedside and took her brother's hand.

James brought over one of the two chairs for Jac to sit in before stepping back up against the sterile white wall to give her some private time with her brother.

He counted the multiple IV bags of different sizes that hung from two poles attached at the head of Ross's bed. Machines ticked and beeped, and the nurse came and went every ten minutes. Ross looked pale and weak, nothing like the vibrant man James had come to know so intimately. If it were the last thing James ever did, he would make sure Ross returned to that man.

"Will you sit with him while I go check on Becca?" Jac asked as she stood.

"Of course." James didn't plan on going anywhere other than Ross's side for a long, long time.

James settled into the chair and took hold of Ross's lacerated hand. He'd used the razor they'd hidden to cut his way free, but came away with some serious contusions. "You know, you scared the hell out of me? You're the first person other than Finn who has had that kind of power over me." He glanced around to make sure no one was listening to him. "I don't like it. Now wake the hell up so we can get on with your recovery." He needed to see those crystal blue eyes again, and hear Ross lecture him about some asinine shit he had done.

"I love you, damn it," James admitted again in case Ross hadn't heard it when they were in the tent.

"I love you...too," Ross's scratchy voice almost sent James falling over backward in his chair.

"You're awake. Doc said you would recover, so do not worry about a thing. I will take care of everything. You get better. That's all you have to do right now." James was rambling, but he couldn't stop himself.

"That's exceptionally responsible of you." Ross's lip turned up in a small smile.

"Bite me, Detective." James smiled back. "You made me like this, now you're going to have to live with it."

"You have such an amazing bedside manner," Ross rasped out, surprising James that he had the strength to keep up the banter.

James stood and placed both of his hands on either side of Ross's head. "Oh, I think you're going to like my bedside manner just fine, Detective." He leaned down and gently kissed Ross's split lips.

"Yeah, I could get used to that," Ross mumbled.

"So could I." James realized as he said it that it was the absolute truth.

No, he had not dealt with all his demons, but with Ross at his side, James thought he might have a fighting chance of making it to the other side of happy.

EPILOGUE

Ross rested against the pile of cushions James had placed behind his back. After being released from the hospital four days ago, Ross had yet to see his handsome soldier sit down or rest. When he woke in the morning, James was already up and in the kitchen preparing breakfast. Even though he fought it, Ross couldn't help the exhaustion that hit him in the afternoons, and, inevitably, he fell off, napping for a couple of hours. James seemed to know the minute Ross stirred, and appeared with water, soup, or a sandwich.

His sister laughed when he'd tried to get her to intervene. She took great joy in reminding him that he'd bitched and moaned that he'd wanted James to be more responsible. Yeah, that was coming back to bite him in the ass. Ross didn't mind James helping him, but the man took his duty to a whole new level. He'd been waiting on Ross hand and foot even when he'd been in the hospital, clearly not pleased with the care the nursing staff was providing.

At the moment, James was out grocery shopping…grocery shopping for Christ sakes. The man hadn't even known where the closest grocery store was located, let alone finding everything on the list Jac had handed him. He'd been gone for hours and Ross was ready to send out a search and rescue team.

"Thank me," Jac said as she walked into the living room.

"What should I thank you for?" Ross asked knowing something was up. "What'd you do?"

Jac plopped down on the couch beside him, causing the springs to jar his healing wounds. Ross couldn't contain his hiss of pain.

"Oh shit, I'm sorry. I wasn't even thinking. Do you need anything?" Jac's earlier smile was replaced by worry. Ross didn't want that. They'd all done enough worrying to last a lifetime.

"No, I'm fine. It didn't hurt that much," Ross told her. "Now out with it. What'd you do?"

Her smile was back in place as she moved closer. "I know James has been driving you nuts, so I made the grocery list super long and added some specialty items to give you some alone time."

"You sneaky little bugger." Ross laughed and held his side to keep the pull on his stitches to a minimum.

"Well, we'll see how happy you are when he gets back with the squid, and you're eating calamari for a week."

"Ewww," Ross grumbled while thinking of those inky bastards squiggling around in his stomach. "Does our grocery store even carry that?"

"Nope," Jac answered with a cheeky grin. "That was the point."

Okay, he'd shove down a few pieces if he had to. "Not complaining here, but I wish James would pull back a little on the hovering, that's all. It's like he's expecting something horrible to happen or some shit."

"Of course. He's scared. So am I. We almost lost you."

"I get that, really, but I'm better now and healing here at home," Ross stated.

"It's hard to get the vision of you covered in blood out of our minds. I never want to go through that again," Jac told him as she sat straighter and then trembled as if she'd felt a chill.

"Neither do I," Ross admitted before taking his sister's hand.

"But I have to admit," Jac shook her head, "James has left me in the dust with his worrying. Hell, he wouldn't leave the hospital, even after they kicked him out of your room so that he would go home and get some rest. Instead, he went to sit in one of the chairs down the hall."

Ross remembered James never being too far away, but he'd had no idea the guy had never left. The guy had to be exhausted and running on fumes. This had to stop. "I wish I had known."

"James wouldn't have listened to you. He's a man on a mission, and that mission is assuring you had and have the best care possible to heal," Jac explained.

"I have a plan to make James rest whether he likes it or not," Ross announced.

Jac got that shifty look in her eyes. "What do you need me to do?"

***

James juggled the grocery bags in his arms in search of his key to Ross's house. It had taken a hell of a lot longer then he imagined finding all the stuff on Jac's list. He had no idea what she intended to do with the slimy eight-legged monster he'd been forced to go to three stores to find, but he was sure he wouldn't be hungry that day.

Thankfully, before he set the bags down on the deck, Jac opened the door. "There you are. I was getting worried."

"Your list was a minefield of shit I've never heard of before. What the hell are you going to be making?"

"Oh, I saw some amazing recipes online that I wanted to give a try."

"Can you try them when I'm not around? I'm not sure my stomach could take it." He set the bags down on the kitchen table.

"I thought you Army boys had steel stomachs."

"There's not enough steel to take on board whatever you're planning on cooking up. Meat and potatoes, that's the good stuff."

"Don't worry your pretty little head, you'll love it," Jac assured, but he doubted he would be able to even withstand the smell. "Ross is lying down in his bedroom and wanted to see you when you got back."

Warning bells went off in his head. "Is he okay? Did something happen while I was gone?" If so, he'd never forgive himself.

"No, no, he's fine. I'll take care of the groceries while you go and see what he wants," Jac said as she pulled the bag holding those slippery suckers from the larger grocery bag. A look of disgust crossed her face making James wonder why she even had him pick it up.

There was no time to puzzle that out. He had to go help Ross. James turned and headed down the short hallway to the master suite. When he opened the door he found Ross resting on the bed, his eyes open.

"Hey, babe. Jac said you wanted to see me. Anything I can get you?" Even though he'd been running around the city for the past couple of hours, he would go out again if Ross wanted something they didn't have.

Ross patted the mattress. "Come lay down with me for a minute. We need to talk."

There weren't many other words that could strike fear into a person quite like, "We need to talk."

"Okay." His mind was racing with possibilities. Was Ross getting sicker? Did he need James to do more to help?

Carefully, he slid onto the bed beside Ross, cautious of jostling his wounds. Once he got settled he asked," What's going on?"

"Close your eyes," Ross ordered. James closed his eyes, and in a split second he felt the pull of sleep. He refused to give in. There was too much to do.

He could feel Ross moving around but it wasn't until he heard that familiar click that he opened his eyes. James looked down at the handcuff around his right wrist and found the other side connected to Ross's left wrist.

What the hell?

Ross smiled with that cocky grin before saying, "Now you'll have to rest."

"What? I'm fine. This is crazy." James tugged lightly at the cuff. It wasn't as if he was being restrained. No reason to freak, but what was Ross playing at?

"You're not fine. You haven't been sleeping and you've been waiting on me since the hospital," Ross told him. "Don't get me wrong, I'm grateful, but you need to slow down before you fall down."

"I rest." James tried his best to sound convincing.

"Yeah? When? Was it during the time at the hospital when you wouldn't leave the building, or was it when you were helping me all day every day? Shit, you're out of bed before I even wake up."

"So? I want to take care of you."

Ross looked at him far too closely for James to hide what he'd been thinking and feeling. "None of this is your fault. Without you, I would have lost Jac and Becca. You've been right by my side through all of this."

"But if I hadn't dropped my gun–"

"If you hadn't dropped your gun there would have been a bullet in my head instead of my stomach. There's no way to come back from that. I got off lucky."

"Lucky? You almost died."

"Yes, almost. But I didn't, and it's time for you to move on from that. I'm not going anywhere." Ross reached for James's hand. "I plan to be around chasing your fine ass for many years.

James couldn't think of anything to say to that. Had he been living in fear of Ross dying, instead of rejoicing in the fact that he was still alive? Damn, he was tired. Maybe his sexy detective had a point.

"Okay. I admit, I might have been overly cautious."

"Cautious, hell, you would have wrapped me in bubble wrap if you could have gotten away with it."

"You can order them by the case online," James shared.

"Of course you would know that," Ross shot back before smiling. "I love you. Now lay down and get some sleep because I'm not planning on moving."

James couldn't help but grin back. "I love you too, Detective." Then he lay down beside the man who came out of nowhere and changed James's entire life for the better. "I still can't believe you cuffed me."

"Hey, I told you from the beginning, I'd use them if I had too." The memory of that night in the bar seemed to be so long ago. "I've gotta admit, I had imagined using them in more pleasurable pursuits, but this will do...for now."

James closed his eyes for what felt like the first time in weeks and drifted off to sleep to the sound of his lover breathing.

Which was perfect.

TAKE A Sneak Peek from Book Four in the Gates of Heaven series: Joey

Joey wiped down the bar as he watched the party get underway. Detective Ross was still recovering from his gunshot wound but it had been over a month since he had been released from the hospital. Every time Joey had seen him he had looked better than the time before.

Joey had been working at The Gates as a bartender for the last six months and he loved his job. The bosses were honest and fair. The rest of the staff seemed to be working out fine, and Marian had taken Joey under her wing.

"Hey, can I have that bottle of champagne for Ross, please?" Finn asked from the other end of the bar.

"Sure, boss. I can bring it over to the table along with glasses if you'd like. And I'll bring some sparkling apple juice for Becca." Joey had to look up at almost everyone who worked at The Gates, what with him being five foot five.

"You're an angel. You think of everything. Thank you," Finn praised before walking back to his group of friends.

There were people in suits, police officers popping in and out to give their best wishes, and a group that looked better suited to the country than the city. Everyone was so happy to have Ross still living in the world beside them. Joey couldn't blame any of them. Ross had always been a straight-up guy. Treated people with respect and had always said hello to Joey when he came to The Gates.

Joey couldn't help but be a little bit jealous, and he felt horrible for it. He couldn't think of a single person that would do the same for him. Especially, if they found out who he really was. That was why he began bartending. It was the perfect job. No one really noticed the person slinging drinks. Customers would talk about their lives and their woes to their heart's content, and not one had asked Joey about himself. Well, maybe the bosses, but they were running the place and needed the information when he was hired. They never pried though, but they'd made it clear they were there for him if he needed.

He'd charged his name for that exact reason, anonymity. Joey was not part of the life his family had forged. Never had been and never would be. He had sworn on his mother's deathbed and he would die before breaking that oath.

Joey wrapped the bottle of Dom Perignon with a starched white napkin then placed it in the standing ice bucket. On a tray, he put sparkling apple juice and half a dozen champagne flutes, and then headed over to the tables. He never uncorked the champagne. Typically, one of the guests wanted to do it, and frequently not right away.

The restaurant had been shut down for the occasion, which Joey didn't mind. It would be a quiet shift before he had to go home. He pushed down that sick feeling he often got at the thought of returning to his empty apartment.

"Ah, he we go. It's not a celebration without champagne," Saint announced as Joey set the bucket alongside the table, then took off the glasses and apple juice and placed them on the table.

"Do you mind opening that for us, Joey?" his other boss, Saint, asked.

"I thought you might like the honor, boss," Joey suggested.

"You're a part of The Gates crew. Did you bring yourself a glass?" Saint was always so generous.

"No sir." Joey could feel the warmth of acceptance seeping into his cold bones.

"Well, let's open that up and then you go grab yourself a glass," Finn ordered. The smallest boss was amazing. He never gave out orders unless it was for your own good. Joey liked and respected him, and worked twice as hard to please him.

"Yes, sir," Joey agreed. The bosses used to try to get him to call them by their first names, but he refused and thankfully they'd stopped trying. His mother taught him to respect those who worked hard and made a good life for themselves.

He removed the foil and muselet from around the top of the bottle and cork. He wrapped a cloth around the top of the bottle and began pulling as he turned the cork. He could feel everyone's eyes on him, which made him shake a little. It must have been enough to lose control of the cork, sending it about ten feet across the room and into the head of one of Ross's fellow police officers.

Joey stood frozen to the spot, his heart beating frantically. "I'm so sorry." Holy shit. He'd ruined the party. Now the cops would look into him.

After a few long moments, Ross broke out laughing. "That'll teach you to keep your eyes open, Webb."

Officer Webb laughed, and so did everyone else. Thank God. Joey quickly set the bottle down. "I'll get you some ice for your head."

He raced back to the safety of his bar, grabbed a plastic bag and filled it with crushed ice. When he turned around, he saw that Officer Webb had followed him and he was now standing on the other side of the bar with a glass of champagne in his hand.

Joey wrapped the bag of ice in a clean towel and handed it to his victim. "I am truly sorry. I don't know what happened." Of course he knew what happened. He had been the center of attention and lost his shit, once again.

The officer smiled, which seemed to light up his face. "Call me Sam, and don't worry about it, accidents happen. This is for you." Webb handed him the glass of champagne

"I was nervous." *Why did I say that?*

"I could tell. I'm guessing you don't like having all eyes on you."

Was he that obvious? "No. I'd rather stay in the background."

"Someone as handsome as you in the background, that might be near impossible and a damned shame," Officer Webb said. "Thanks to your shot, I found a reason to talk to you."

Joey could feel his cheeks warming and he knew he was blushing. *I am such a child.* His birth certificate might say he was twenty-eight, but his behavior led people to believe he had barely broke eighteen.

Sam took the ice pack and held it to the side of his head before reaching into his shirt pocket.

"I'll let you make it up to me," he said as he placed his business card on the bar top. "Let me take you out for coffee sometime and we will call it even."

"How is that making it up to you if you're the one paying for the coffee?" Joey asked.

Sam smiled and Joey could feel his heart speeding up.

"Because you will save me from drinking coffee all alone. Think about it." Sam winked and turned to rejoin the party.

Did Officer Webb just ask him out on a date? Wouldn't that send dear old granddad over the edge. Joey tucked the card into the pocket of his pants and went back to cleaning the bar.

He sure as certain was interested, but that coffee rendezvous could never happen. Joey had to keep his secret safe and dating a cop was the absolute wrong thing to assure that continued to happen.

But, there was no harm in dreaming.

ABOUT THE AUTHOR

M. Tasia lives in a small town in Ontario, Canada. She's a member of the Romance Writers of America, and its Rainbow Romance Writers and Toronto Romance Writers chapters. Michelle is a dedicated people-watcher, lover of romance novels, '80s rock, and happy endings. Also, she's the mother of two wonderful girls, wife to a great husband, and new grandmother, as well as servant to two spoiled furry children who don't seem to realize that they're actually cats.

Michelle writes contemporary and paranormal romance, and she believes love should be celebrated. After all, everybody needs a little romance, excitement, intrigue, and passion in their lives.

Connect with Michelle:
mtasiabooks.com
facebook.com/mtasiabooks
twitter.com/mtasiaauthor
instagram.com/m.tasia.author/

www.BOROUGHSPUBLISHINGGROUP.com

If you enjoyed this book, please write a review. Our authors appreciate the feedback, and it helps future readers find books they love. We welcome your comments and invite you to send them to info@boroughspublishinggroup.com. Follow us on Facebook, Twitter and Instagram, and be sure to sign up for our newsletter for surprises and new releases from your favorite authors.

Are you an aspiring writer? Check out www.boroughspublishinggroup.com/submit and see if we can help you make your dreams come true.

www.ingramcontent.com/pod-product-compliance
Lightning Source LLC
Chambersburg PA
CBHW030315130626
46549CB00002B/864